當代中文課程

A Course in
Contemporary
Chinese

編寫教師・王佩卿、陳慶華、黃桂英

主編・鄧守信

二版

Textbook

|課本|

1-2

國立臺灣師範大學國語教學中心 策劃
Mandarin Training Center National Taiwan Normal University

# 序　Foreword

　　臺灣師範大學國語教學中心成立於 1956 年，是臺灣歷史最悠久、規模最完備、教學最有成效的華語文教學機構。每年培育三千名以上的外籍學生，學生來自世界一百二十餘國，至今累計人數已達五萬餘人，在國際間享譽盛名。

　　本中心自 1967 年開始編製教材，迄今共計編寫五十餘本教材，在華語教學界具有舉足輕重之地位。而現今使用之主教材已有十五年之久，不少學生及教師認為現行教材內容需要更新，應新編配合時代需求的新教材。因此，本中心因應外在環境變遷、教學法及教學媒體的創新與進步，籌畫編寫《當代中文課程》6 冊，以符合海內外華語教學的需求，並強化臺灣華語文教學教材之品牌。

　　為了讓理論與實務結合，並落實發揚華語文教學的精神與理念，本中心邀請了華語教學界的大師——鄧守信教授擔任主編，率領 18 位極富教學經驗的第一線老師進行內容編寫，並由張莉萍副研究員、張黛琪老師及教材研發組成員蔡如珮、張雯雯擔任執行編輯，進行了這項《當代中文課程》的編寫計畫。

　　這是本中心歷經數十年深厚教學經驗後再次開發的全新主教材，更為了確保品質，特別慎重；我們很榮幸地邀請到美國的 Claudia Ross 教授、白建華教授及陳雅芬教授，擔任顧問，也邀請了臺灣的葉德明教授、美國的姚道中教授及大陸的劉珣教授，擔任審查委員，並由本校英語系李櫻教授和畢永峨教授分別協助生詞和語法的翻譯。此教材在本中心及臺灣其他語言中心，進行了一年多的試用；經過顧問的悉心指導、審查委員的仔細批閱，並參考了老師及學生提出的寶貴意見，再由編寫老師做了多次修改，才將版本定稿。對於所有在編寫過程中，努力不懈的編輯團隊、給予指教的教授、配合試用的老師及學生，我們都要致上最高的謝意。

　　在此也特別感謝聯經出版事業股份有限公司，願意投注最大的心力，以專業的製作出版能力，協助我們將這套教材以最佳品質問世。

　　我們希望，《當代中文課程》不只提供學生們一套實用有效的教材，亦讓老師得到愉快充實的教學經驗。歡迎老師在使用後，給予我們更多的指教與建議，讓我們不斷進步，也才能為海內外的華語教學，做更多更好的貢獻。

臺灣師範大學國語教學中心主任　陳浩然

The Mandarin Training Center (MTC) at National Taiwan Normal University (NTNU) was established in 1956, and is the oldest, most comprehensive, and most pedagogically effective educational institute of its kind in Taiwan. Every year over 3,000 international students are trained at MTC, and to the present day over 50,000 students representing more than 120 countries have walked through its doors, solidifying international renown.

MTC started producing teaching material in 1967, and has since completed over 50 textbooks, making it a frontrunner in the field of teaching Chinese as a second language. As the core books have been in circulation for 15 years already, many students and teachers agree that updates are in order, and that new materials should be made to meet the modern demand. Changes in the social landscape, improved teaching methods, and innovations in educational media are what prompted the production of MTC's six-volume series, *A Course in Contemporary Chinese*. The project responds to Chinese teaching needs both at home and abroad, and bolsters Taiwan's brand of teaching material for Chinese as a second language.

With the goal of integrating theory and practice, and carrying forward the spirit of teaching Chinese as a second language, MTC petitioned one of the field's most esteemed professors, Shou-Hsin Teng, to serve as chief editor. *A Course in Contemporary Chinese* has been compiled and edited under his leadership, together with the help of 18 seasoned Chinese teachers and the following four executive editors: Associate Research Fellow Liping Chang, Tai-chi Chang, and Ru-pei Cai and Wen-wen Chang of the MTC teaching material development division.

MTC is presenting this brand new core material after half a century's worth of educational experience, and we have taken extra care to ensure it is of uncompromised quality. We were delighted to have American professors Claudia Ross, Jianhua Bai , and Yea-fen Chen act as consultants, Professor Teh-Ming Yeh from Taiwan, Professor Tao-chung Yao from the U.S., and Professor Xun Liu from China on the review committee, and professors Ying Cherry Li and Yung-O Biq of NTNU's English department help with the respective translation of vocabulary and grammar points. The material was first trialed at MTC and other language centers around Taiwan for a year. The current version underwent numerous drafts, and materialized under the careful guidance of the consultants, a sedulous reading from the review committee, and feedback from teachers and students. As for the editorial process, we owe the greatest thanks to the indefatigable editorial team, the professors and their invaluable input, and the teachers and students who were willing to trial the book.

An additional and special thanks is due to Linking Publishing Company, who put forth utmost effort and professionalism in publishing this set of teaching material, allowing us to deliver a publication of superior quality.

It is our hope that *A Course in Contemporary Chinese* is not merely a practical set of teaching materials for students, but also enriching for teachers and the entire teaching experience. We welcome comments from instructors who have put the books into practice so that we can continue improving the material. Only then can we keep furthering our contribution to the field of teaching Chinese as a second language, both in Taiwan and abroad.

**Hao Jan Chen**
Director of the Mandarin Training Center
National Taiwan Normal University

# From the Editor's Desk

主編的話

Finally, after more than two years, volume one of our six-volume project is seeing the light of day. The language used in *A Course in Contemporary Chinese* is up to date, and though there persists a deep 'generation gap' between it and my own brand of Chinese, this is as it should be. In addition to myself, our project team has consisted of 18 veteran MTC teachers and the entire staff of the MTC Section of Instructional Materials, plus the MTC Deputy Director.

The field of L2 Chinese in Taiwan seems to have adopted the world-famous 'one child policy'. The complete set of currently used textbooks was born a generation ago, and until now has been without predecessor. We are happy to fill this vacancy, and with the title 'number two', yet we also aspire to have it be number two in name alone. After a generation, we present a slightly disciplined contemporary language as observed in Taiwan, we employ Hanyu Pinyin without having to justify it cautiously and timidly, we are proud to present a brand-new system of Chinese parts of speech that will hopefully eliminate many instances of error, we have devised two kinds of exercises in our series, one basically structural and the other entirely task-based, each serving its own intended function, and finally we have included in each lesson a special aspect of Chinese culture. Moreover, all this is done in full color, the first time ever in the field of L2 Chinese in Taiwan. The settings for our current series is in Taipei, Taiwan, with events taking place near the National Taiwan Normal University. The six volumes progress from basic colloquial to semi-formal and finally to authentic conversations or narratives. The glossary in vocabulary and grammar is in basically semi-literal English, not free translation, as we wish to guide the readers/learners along the Chinese 'ways of thinking', but rest assured that no pidgin English has been used.

I am a functional, not structural, linguist, and users of our new textbooks will find our approaches and explanations more down to earth. Both teachers and learners will find that the content resonates with their own experiences and feelings. Rote learning plays but a tiny part of our learning experiences. In a functional frame, the role of the speaker often seen as prominent. This is natural, as numerous adverbs in Chinese, as they are traditionally referred to, do not in fact modify verb phrases at all. They relate to the speaker.

We, the field of Chinese as a second language, know a lot about how to teach, especially when it comes to Chinese characters. Most L2 Chinese teachers world-wide are ethnically Chinese, and teach characters just as they were taught in childhood. Truth is, we know next to nothing how adult students/learners actually learn characters, and other elements of the Chinese language. While we have nothing new in this series of textbooks that contributes to the teaching of Chinese characters, I tried to tightly integrate teaching and learning through our presentation of vocabulary items and grammatical structures. Underneath such methodologies is my personal conviction, and at times both instructors' and learners' patience is requested. I welcome communication with all users of our new textbooks, whether instructors or students/learners.

**Shou-hsin Teng**

## Series Introduction

This six-volume series is a comprehensive learning material that focuses on spoken language in the first three volumes and written language in the latter three volumes. Volume One aims to strengthen daily conversation and applications; Volume Two contains short essays as supplementary readings; Volume Three introduces beginning-level written language and discourse, in addition to extended dialogues. Volume Four uses discourse to solidify the learner's written language and ability in reading authentic materials; Volumes Five and Six are arranged in topics such as society, technology, economics, politics, culture, and environment to help the learner expand their language utilizations in different domains.

Each volume includes a textbook, a student workbook, and a teacher's manual. In addition, Volume One and Two include a practice book for characters.

## Level of Students

*A Course in Contemporary Chinese*《當代中文課程》is suitable for learners of Chinese in Taiwan, as well as for high school or college level Chinese language courses overseas. Volumes One to Six cover levels A1 to C1 in the CEFR, or Novice to Superior levels in ACTFL Guidelines.

## Overview

- The series adopts communicative language teaching and task-based learning to boost the learner's Chinese ability.

- Each lesson has learning objectives and self-evaluation to give the learner a clear record of tasks completed.

- Lessons are authentic daily situations to help the learner learn in natural contexts.

- Lexical items and syntactic structures are presented and explained in functional, not structural, perspectives.

- Syntactic, i.e. grammatical, explanation includes functions, structures, pragmatics, and drills to guide the learner to proper usage.

- Classroom activities have specific learning objectives, activities, or tasks to help fortify learning while having fun.

- The "Bits of Chinese Culture" section of the lesson has authentic photographs to give the learner a deeper look at local Taiwanese culture.

- Online access provides supplementary materials for teachers & students.

# 改版緣起 Reasons for the Revision

　　《當代中文課程》第一冊出版迄今已六年，在中華文化中，「六」這個數字象徵著吉祥，也代表了和諧融洽的意涵。我們將六年以來所接獲的各方意見，彙整之後進行教材改版，希望能藉由教材的新面貌，答謝讀者這些日子以來對《當代中文課程》的支持與愛護。

　　新版《當代中文課程》在紙本教材方面，不僅修訂教材內容，也調整了分冊形式，便於讀者攜帶；在數位方面則改善了音檔下載的使用流程，讓操作更加流暢。此外，我們為每課對話製作擴增實境（Augmented Reality，簡稱 AR）動畫，增添教材的數位互動性。讀者只需將行動裝置（手機或平板）掃描課本中的課文插圖，就能看到生動的動畫。文字搭配動態圖像使學習更富樂趣，並有助於強化記憶，自然而然地提升學習成效。

　　《當代中文課程》編著團隊致力於落實「當代」之名，讓此套教材在任何時刻都順應潮流，符合當代語彙，符合當代中文學習者的使用需求。以此考量，推出新版《當代中文課程》，若未來讀者有任何新期許，也歡迎繼續賜教。

　　It has been six years since the first volume of *A Course in Contemporary Chinese* was published. For Chinese culture, the number "six" symbolizes good luck and also means harmony and rapport. We have further consolidated the diverse opinions we have received over the past six years and then revised the teaching materials. With the new look of textbooks, we are eager to thank readers for their support and love to *A Course in Contemporary Chinese* over the past few years.

　　In terms of paper textbooks, the new edition of *A Course in Contemporary Chinese* has not only revised the content of the textbooks, but also adjusted the format to several volumes to make it easy for readers to carry. Regarding the digital aspect, the use process of audio file download has been optimized to make the operation smoother. On top of that, we create augmented reality (AR for short) animations for the dialogues of each lesson, which adds to the digital interactivity of the teaching materials. Therefore, readers only need to scan the text illustrations in the textbook with their mobile devices (mobile phones or tablets) to see vivid animations. Based on this, this textbook is composed of text and dynamic images to make learning more fun, and helps strengthen readers' memory and promote learning effectiveness.

　　The editorial team of *A Course in Contemporary Chinese* is dedicated to implementing the name "Contemporary," hoping to make this set of textbooks follow the trend of the generation at all times and meet the needs of contemporary vocabulary and contemporary Chinese learners. In view of this, we launched a new version of *A Course in Contemporary Chinese*. If future readers have any new related expectations, please continue to remind us.

1. 使用行動裝置（手機或平板）免費下載 MAKAR APP （僅限 iOS 及 Android 系統）
   Readers are invited to use mobile devices (mobile phones or tablets) to download MAKAR APP for free (iOS and Android systems only).

App Store (iOS)　　　　Google Play (Android)

2. 開啟 MAKAR APP
   Enable MAKAR APP

❶ 點擊「搜尋」　　　　　　　　　　Click "Search"

❷ 於搜尋欄位中輸入「Dangdai」　　Enter "Dangdai" in the search field

❸ 點擊「專案」　　　　　　　　　　Click "Project"

❹ 點擇任一專案（無須對照課數）　　Click any project (no need to match the number of courses)

❺ 點擊「開始體驗」　　　　　　　　Click "Start Experience"

❻ 掃描《當代中文課程》課本的課文插圖即可播放動畫
   Scan the illustrations of the text in the textbook of *A Course in Contemporary Chinese* to start playing the animation.

# An Introduction to the Chinese Language

China is a multi-ethnic society, and when people in general study Chinese, 'Chinese' usually refers to the Beijing variety of the language as spoken by the Han people in China, also known as Mandarin Chinese or simply Mandarin. It is the official language of China, known mostly domestically as the Putonghua, the lingua franca, or Hanyu, the Han language. In Taiwan, Guoyu refers to the national/official language, and Huayu to either Mandarin Chinese as spoken by Chinese descendants residing overseas, or to Mandarin when taught to non-Chinese learners. The following pages present an outline of the features and properties of Chinese. For further details, readers are advised to consult various and rich on-line resources.

## Language Kinship

Languages in the world are grouped together on the basis of language affiliation, called language-family. Chinese, or rather Hanyu, is a member of the Sino-Tibetan family, which covers most of China today, plus parts of Southeast Asia. Therefore, Tibetan, Burmese, and Thai are genetically related to Hanyu.

Hanyu is spoken in about 75% of the present Chinese territory, by about 75% of the total Chinese population, and it covers 7 major dialects, including the better known Cantonese, Hokkienese, Hakka and Shanghainese.

Historically, Chinese has interacted highly actively with neighboring but unaffiliated languages, such as Japanese, Korean and Vietnamese. The interactions took place in such areas as vocabulary items, phonological structures, a few grammatical features and most importantly the writing script.

## Typological Features of Chinese

Languages in the world are also grouped together on the basis of language characteristics, called language typology. Chinese has the following typological traits, which highlight the dissimilarities between Chinese and English.

**A. Chinese is a non-tense language.** Tense is a grammatical device such that the verb changes according to the time of the event in relation to the time of utterance. Thus 'He talks nonsense' refers to his habit, while 'He talked nonsense' refers to a time in the past when he behaved that way, but he does not necessarily do that all the time. 'Talked' then is a verb in the past tense. Chinese does not operate with this device but marks the time of events with time expressions such as 'today' or 'tomorrow' in the sentence. The verb remains the same regardless of time of happening. This type of language is labeled as an atensal language, while English and most European languages are tensal languages. Knowing this particular trait can help European learners of Chinese avoid mistakes to do with verbs in Chinese. Thus, in responding to 'What did you do in China last year?' Chinese is 'I teach English (last year)'; and to 'What are you doing now in Japan?' Chinese is again 'I teach English (now)'.

**B. Nouns in Chinese are not directly countable.** Nouns in English are either countable, e.g. 2 candies, or non-countable, e.g. *2 salts, while all nouns in Chinese are non-countable. When they are to be counted, a measure, or called classifier, must be used between a noun and a number, e.g. 2-piece-candy. Thus, Chinese is a classifier language. Only non-countable nouns in English are used with measures, e.g. a drop of water.

Therefore it is imperative to learn nouns in Chinese together with their associated measures/classifiers. There are only about 30 high-frequency measures/classifiers in Chinese to be mastered at the initial stage of learning.

**C. Chinese is a Topic-Prominent language.** Sentences in Chinese quite often begin with somebody or something that is being talked about, rather than the subject of the verb in the sentence. This item is called a topic in linguistics. Most Asian languages employ topic, while most European languages employ subject. The following bad English sentences, sequenced below per frequency of usage, illustrate the topic structures in Chinese.

*Senator Kennedy, people in Europe also respected.

*Seafood, Taiwanese people love lobsters best.

*President Obama, he attended Harvard University.

Because of this feature, Chinese people tend to speak 'broken' English, whereas English speakers tend to sound 'complete', if bland and alien, when they talk in Chinese. Through practice and through keen observations of what motivates the use of a topic in Chinese, this feature of Chinese can be acquired eventually.

**D. Chinese tends to drop things in the sentence.** The 'broken' tendencies mentioned above also include not using nouns in a sentence where English counterparts are 'complete'. This tendency is called dropping, as illustrated below through bad English sentences.

Are you coming tomorrow? ----- *Come!

What did you buy? ----- *Buy some jeans.

*This bicycle, who rides? ----- *My old professor rides.

The 1st example drops everything except the verb, the 2nd drops the subject, and the 3rd drops the object. Dropping happens when what is dropped is easily recoverable or identifiable from the contexts or circumstances. Not doing this, Europeans are often commented upon that their sentences in Chinese are too often inundated with unwanted pronouns!!

## Phonological Characteristics of Chinese

Phonology refers to the system of sound, the pronunciation, of a language. To untrained ears, Chinese language sounds unfamiliar, sort of alien in a way. This is due to the fact that Chinese sound system contains some elements that are not part of the sound systems of European languages, though commonly found on the Asian continent. These features will be explained below.

On the whole, the Chinese sound system is not really very complicated. It has 7 vowels, 5 of which are found in English (i, e, a, o, u), plus 2 which are not (-e,); and it has 21 consonants, 15 of which are quite common, plus 6 which are less common (zh, ch, sh, r, z, c). And Chinese has a fairly simple syllable shape, i.e. consonant + vowel  plus possible nasals (n or ng). What is most striking to English speakers is that every syllable in Chinese has a 'tone', as will be detailed directly below. But, a word on the sound representation, the pinyin system, first.

**A. Hanyu Pinyin.** Hanyu Pinyin is a variety of Romanization systems that attempt to represent the sound of Chinese through the use of Roman letters (abc...). Since the end of the 19th century, there have been about half a dozen Chinese Romanization systems, including the Wade-Giles, Guoyu Luomazi, Yale, Hanyu Pinyin, Lin Yutang, and Zhuyin Fuhao Di'ershi, not to mention the German system, the French system etc. Thanks to the consensus of media worldwide, and through the support of the UN, Hanyu Pinyin has become the standard worldwide. Taiwan is probably the only place in the world that does not support nor employ Hanyu Pinyin. Instead, it uses non-Roman symbols to represent the sound, called Zhuyin Fuhao, alias BoPoMoFo (cf. the symbols employed in this volume). Officially, that is. Hanyu Pinyin represents the Chinese sound as follows.

b, p, m, f    d, t, n, l    g, k, h    j, q, x    zh, ch, sh, r    z, c, s

a, o, -e, e    ai, ei, ao, ou    an, en, ang, eng    -r, i, u, ü

**B. Chinese is a tonal language.** A tone refers to the voice pitch contour. Pitch contours are used in many languages, including English, but for different functions in different languages. English uses them to indicate the speaker's viewpoints, e.g. 'well' in different contours may indicate impatience, surprise, doubt etc. Chinese, on the other hand, uses contours to refer to different meanings, words. Pitch contours with different linguistic functions are not transferable from one language to another. Therefore, it would be futile trying to learn Chinese tones by looking for or identifying their contour counterparts in English.

Mandarin Chinese has 4 distinct tones, the fewest among all Han dialects, i.e. level, rising, dipping and falling, marked ‾ ╱ ╲ ╲, and it has only one tone-change rule, i.e. ╲ ╲ → ╱ ╲, though the conditions for this change are fairly complicated. In addition to the four tones, Mandarin also has one neutral(ized) tone, i.e.·, pronounced short/unstressed, which is derived, historically if not synchronically, from the 4 tones; hence the term neutralized. Again, the conditions and environments for the neutralization are highly complex and cannot be explored in this space.

**C. Syllable final –r effect (vowel retroflexivisation).** The northern variety of Hanyu, esp. in Beijing, is known for its richness in the –r effect at the end of a syllable. For example, 'flower' is 'huā' in southern China but 'huār' in Beijing. Given the prominence of the city Beijing, this sound feature tends to be defined as standard nationwide; but that –r effect is rarely attempted in the south. There do not seem to be rigorous rules governing what can and what cannot take the –r effect. It is thus advised that learners of Chinese resort to rote learning in this case, as probably even native speakers of northern Chinese do.

**D. Syllables in Chinese do not 'connect'.** 'Connect' here refers to the merging of the tail of a syllable with the head of a subsequent syllable, e.g. English pronounces 'at' + 'all' as 'at+tall', 'did' +'you' as 'did+dyou' and 'that'+'is' as 'that+th'is'. On the other hand, syllables in Chinese are isolated from each other and do not connect in this way. Fortunately, this is not a serious problem for English language learners, as the syllable structures in Chinese are rather limited, and there are not many candidates for this merging. We noted above that Chinese syllables take the form of CV plus possible 'n' and 'ng'. CV does not give rise to connecting, not even in English; so be extra cautious when a syllable ends with 'n' or 'g' and a subsequent syllable begins with a V, e.g. MǐnÀo 'Fujian Province and Macao'. Nobody would understand 'min+nao'!!

**E. Retroflexive consonants.** 'Retroflexive' refers to consonants that are pronounced with the tip of the tongue curled up (-flexive) backwards (retro-). There are altogether 4 such consonants, i.e. zh, ch, sh, and r. The pronunciation of these consonants reveals the geographical origin of native Chinese speakers. Southerners do not have them, merging them with z, c, and s, as is commonly observed in Taiwan. Curling up of the tongue comes in various degrees. Local Beijing dialect is well known for its prominent curling. Imagine curling up the tongue at the beginning of a syllable and curling it up again for the –r effect!! ! Try 'zhèr-over here', 'zhuōr-table' and 'shuǐr-water'.

**On Chinese Grammar**

'Grammar' refers to the ways and rules of how words are organized into a string that is a sentence in a language. Given the fact that all languages have sentences, and at the same time non-sentences, all languages including Chinese have grammar. In this section, the most salient and important features and issues of Chinese grammar will be presented, but a summary of basic structures, as referenced against English, is given first.

**A. Similarities in Chinese and English.**

|  | English | Chinese |
|---|---|---|
| SVO | They sell coffee. | Tāmen mài kāfēi. |
| AuxV+Verb | You may sit down! | Nǐ kěyǐ zuòxià ō! |
| Adj+Noun | sour grapes | suān pútáo |
| Prep+its Noun | at home | zài jiā |
| Num+Meas+Noun | a piece of cake | yí kuài dàngāo |
| Demons+Noun | those students | nàxiē xuéshēng |

**B. Dissimilar structures.**

|  | English | Chinese |
|---|---|---|
| RelClause: Noun | the book that you bought | nǐ mǎi de shū |
| VPhrase: PrepPhrase | to eat at home | zài jiā chīfàn |
| Verb: Adverbial | Eat slowly! | Mànmār chī! |

| Set: Subset | 6th Sept, 1967 | 1967 nián 9 yuè 6 hào |
| | Taipei, Taiwan | Táiwān Táiběi |
| | 3 of my friends… | wǒ de péngyǒu, yǒu sān ge… |

**C. Modifier precedes modified (MPM).** This is one of the most important grammatical principles in Chinese. We see it operating actively in the charts given above, so that adjectives come before nouns they modify, relative clauses also come before the nouns they modify, possessives come before nouns (tā de diànnǎo 'his computer'), auxiliary verbs come before verbs, adverbial phrases before verbs, prepositional phrases come before verbs etc. This principle operates almost without exceptions in Chinese, while in English modifiers sometimes precede and some other times follow the modified.

**D. Principle of Temporal Sequence (PTS).** Components of a sentence in Chinese are lined up in accordance with the sequence of time. This principle operates especially when there is a series of verbs contained within a sentence, or when there is a sentential conjunction. First compare the sequence of 'units' of an event in English and that in its Chinese counterpart.

Event: David /went to New York/ by train /from Boston/ to see his sister.

English: 1         2        3        4        5

Chinese: 1        4        2        3        5

Now in real life, David got on a train, the train departed from Boston, it arrived in New York, and finally he visited his sister. This sequence of units is 'natural' time, and the Chinese sentence 'Dàwèi zuò huǒchē cóng Bōshìdùn dào Niǔyuē qù kàn tā de jiějie' follows it, but not English. In other words, Chinese complies strictly with PTS.

When sentences are conjoined, English has various possibilities in organizing the conjunction. First, the scenario. H1N1 hits China badly (event-1), and as a result, many schools were closed (event-2). Now, English has the following possible ways of conjoining to express this, e.g.

Many schools were closed, because/since H1N1 hit China badly. (E2+E1)

H1N1 hit China badly, so many schools were closed. (E1+E2)

As H1N1 hit China badly, many schools were closed. (E1+E2)

Whereas the only way of expressing the same in Chinese is E1+E2 when both conjunctions are used (yīnwèi…suǒyǐ…), i.e.

Zhōngguó yīnwèi H1N1 gǎnrǎn yánzhòng (E1), suǒyǐ xǔduō xuéxiào zhànshí guānbì (E2).

PTS then helps explain why 'cause' is always placed before 'consequence' in Chinese.

PTS is also seen operating in the so-called verb-complement constructions in Chinese, e.g. shā-sǐ 'kill+dead', chī-bǎo 'eat+full', dǎ-kū 'hit+cry' etc. The verb represents an action that must have happened first before its consequence.

There is an interesting group of adjectives in Chinese, namely 'zǎo-early', 'wǎn-late', 'kuài-fast', 'màn-slow', 'duō-plenty', and 'shǎo-few', which can be placed either before (as adverbials) or after (as complements) of their associated verbs, e.g.

Nǐ míngtiān zǎo diǎr lái! (Come earlier tomorrow!)

Wǒ lái zǎo le. Jìnbúqù. (I arrived too early. I could not get in.)

When 'zǎo' is placed before the verb 'lái', the time of arrival is intended, planned, but when it is placed after, the time of arrival is not pre-planned, maybe accidental. The difference complies with PTS. The same difference holds in the case of the other adjectives in the group, e.g.

Qǐng nǐ duō mǎi liǎngge! (Please get two extra!)

Wǒ mǎiduō le. Zāotà le! (I bought two too many. Going to be wasted!)

'Duō' in the first sentence is going to be pre-planned, a pre-event state, while in the second, it's a post-event report. Pre-event and post-event states then are naturally taken care of by PTS. Our last set in the group is more complicated. 'Kuài' and 'màn' can refer to amount of time in addition to manner of action, as illustrated below.

Nǐ kuài diǎr zǒu; yào chídào le! (Hurry up and go! You'll be late (e.g. for work)!)

Qǐng nǐ zǒu kuài yìdiǎr! (Please walk faster!)

'Kuài' in the first can be glossed as 'quick, hurry up' (in as little time as possible after the utterance), while that in the second refers to manner of walking. Similarly, 'màn yìdiǎr zǒu-don't leave yet' and 'zǒu màn yìdiǎr-walk more slowly'.

We have seen in this section the very important role in Chinese grammar played by variations in word-order. European languages exhibit rich resources in changing the forms of verbs, adjectives and nouns, and Chinese, like other Asian languages, takes great advantage of word-order.

**E. Where to find subjects in existential sentences.** Existential sentences refer to sentences in which the verbs express appearing (e.g. coming), disappearing (e.g. going) and presence (e.g. written (on the wall)). The existential verbs are all intransitive, and thus they are all associated with a subject, without any objects naturally. This type of sentences deserves a mention in this introduction, as they exhibit a unique structure in Chinese. When their subjects are in definite reference (something that can be referred to, e.g. pronouns and nouns with definite article in English) the subject appears at the front of the sentence, i.e. before the existential verb, but when their subjects are in indefinite reference (nothing in particular), the subject appears after the verb. Compare the following pair of sentences in Chinese against their counterparts in English.

Kèrén dōu lái le. Chīfàn ba! (All the guests we invited have arrived. Let's serve the dinner.)

Duìbùqǐ! Láiwǎn le. Jiālǐ láile yí ge kèrén. (Sorry for being late! I had an (unexpected) guest.)

More examples of post-verbal subjects are given below.

Zhè cì táifēng sǐle bù shǎo rén. (Quite a few people died during the typhoon this time.)

Zuótiān wǎnshàng xiàle duō jiǔ de yǔ? (How long did it rain last night?)

Zuótiān wǎnshàng pǎole jǐ ge fànrén? (How many inmates got away last night?)

Chēzi lǐ zuòle duōshǎo rén a? (How many people were in the car?)

Exactly when to place the existential subject after the verb will remain a challenge for learners of Chinese for quite a significant period of time. Again, observe and deduce!! Memorising sentence by sentence would not help!!

The existential subjects presented above are simple enough, e.g. people, a guest, rain and inmates. But when the subject is complex, further complications emerge!! A portion of the complex subject stays in front of the verb, and the remaining goes to the back of the verb, e.g.

Míngtiān nǐmen qù jǐge rén? (How many of you will be going tomorrow?)

Wǒ zuìjìn diàole bù shǎo tóufǎ. (I lost=fell quite a lot of hair recently.)

Qùnián dìzhèn, tā sǐle sān ge gēge. (He lost=died 3 brothers during the earthquake last year.)

In linguistics, we say that existential sentences in Chinese have a lot of semantic and information structures involved.

**F. A tripartite system of verb classifications in Chinese.** English has a clear division between verbs and adjectives, but the boundary in Chinese is quite blurred, which quite seriously misleads English-speaking learners of Chinese. The error in *Wǒ jīntiān shì máng. 'I am busy today.' is a daily observation in Chinese 101! Why is it a common mistake for beginning learners? What do our textbooks and/or teachers do about it, so that the error is discouraged, if not suppressed? Nothing, much! What has not been realized in our profession is that Chinese verb classification is more strongly semantic, rather than more strongly syntactic as in English.

Verbs in Chinese have 3 sub-classes, namely Action Verbs, State Verbs and Process Verbs. Action Verbs are time-sensitive activities (beginning and ending, frozen with a snap-shot, prolonged), are will-controlled (consent or refuse), and usually take human subjects, e.g. 'chī-eat', 'mǎi-buy' and 'xué-learn'. State Verbs are non-time-sensitive physical or mental states, inclusive of the all-famous adjectives as a further sub-class, e.g. 'ài-love', 'xīwàng-hope' and 'liàng-bright'. Process Verbs refer to instantaneous change from one state to another, 'sǐ-die', 'pò-break, burst' and 'wán-finish'.

The new system of parts of speech in Chinese as adopted in this series is built on this very foundation of this tripartite verb classification. Knowing this new system will be immensely helpful in learning quite a few syntactic structures in Chinese that are nicely related to the 3 classes of verbs, as will be illustrated with negation in Chinese in the section below.

The table below presents some of the most important properties of these 3 classes of verbs, as reflected through syntactic behaviour.

| | Action Verbs | State Verbs | Process Verbs |
|---|---|---|---|
| Hěn- modification | ✗ | ✓ | ✗ |
| Le- completive | ✓ | ✗ | ✓ |
| Zài- progressive | ✓ | ✗ | ✗ |
| Reduplication | ✓ (tentative) | ✓ (intensification) | ✗ |
| Bù- negation | ✓ | ✓ | ✗ |
| Méi- negation | ✓ | ✗ | ✓ |

Here are more examples of 3 classes of verbs.

Action Verbs: mǎi 'buy', zuò 'sit', xué 'learn; imitate', kàn 'look'

State Verbs: xǐhuān 'like', zhīdào 'know', néng 'can', guì 'expensive'

Process Verbs: wàngle 'forget', chén 'sink', bìyè 'graduate', xǐng 'wake up'

**G. Negation.** Negation in Chinese is by means of placing a negative adverb immediately in front of a verb. (Remember that adjectives in Chinese are a type of State verbs!) When an action verb is negated with 'bu', the meaning can be either 'intend not to, refuse to' or 'not in a habit of', e.g.

Nǐ bù mǎi piào; wǒ jiù bú ràng nǐ jìnqù! (If you don't buy a ticket, I won't let you in!)

Tā zuótiān zhěng tiān bù jiē diànhuà. (He did not want to answer the phone all day yesterday.)

Dèng lǎoshī bù hē jiǔ. (Mr. Teng does not drink.)

'Bù' has the meaning above but is independent of temporal reference. The first sentence above refers to the present moment or a minute later after the utterance, and the second to the past. A habit again is panchronic. But when an action verb is negated with 'méi(yǒu)', its time reference must be in the past, meaning 'something did not come to pass', e.g.

Tā méi lái shàngbān. (He did not come to work.)

Tā méi dài qián lái. (He did not bring any money.)

A state verb can only be negated with 'bù', referring to the non-existence of that state, whether in the past, at present, or in the future, e.g.

Tā bù zhīdào zhèjiàn shì. (He did not/does not know this.)

Tā bù xiǎng gēn nǐ qù. (He did not/does not want to go with you.)

Niǔyuē zuìjìn bú rè. (New York was/is/will not be hot.)

A process verb can only be negated with 'méi', referring to the non-happening of a change from one state to another, usually in the past, e.g.

Yīfú méi pò; nǐ jiù rēng le? (You threw away perfectly good clothes?)

Niǎo hái méi sǐ; nǐ jiù fàng le ba! (The bird is still alive. Why don't you let it free?)

Tā méi bìyè yǐqián, hái děi dǎgōng. (He has to work odd jobs before graduating.)

As can be gathered from the above, negation of verbs in Chinese follows neat patterns, but this is so only after we work with the new system of verb classifications as presented in this series. Here's one more interesting fact about negation in Chinese before closing this section. When some action verbs refer to some activities that result in something stable, e.g. when you put on clothes, you want the clothes to stay on you, the negation of those verbs can be usually translated in the present tense in English, e.g.

Tā zěnme méi chuān yīfú? (How come he is naked?)

Wǒ jīntiān méi dài qián. (I have no money with me today.)

**H. A new system of Parts of Speech in Chinese.** In the system of parts of speech adopted in this series, there are at the highest level a total of 8 parts of speech, as given below. This system includes the following major properties. First and foremost, it is errors-driven and can address some of the most prevailing errors exhibited by learners of Chinese. This characteristic dictates the depth of sub-categories in a system of grammatical categories. Secondly, it employs the concept of 'default'. This property greatly simplifies the over-all framework of the new system, so that it reduces the number of categories used, simplifies the labeling of categories, and takes advantage of the learners' contribution in terms of positive transfer. And lastly, it incorporates both semantic as well as syntactic concepts, so that it bypasses the traditionally problematic category of adjectives by establishing three major semantic types of verbs, viz. action, state and process.

| | |
|---|---|
| Adv | Adverb (dōu 'all', dàgài 'probably') |
| Conj | Conjunction (gēn 'and', kěshì 'but') |
| Det | Determiner (zhè 'this', nà 'that') |
| M | Measure (ge, tiáo; xià, cì) |
| N | Noun (wǒ 'I', yǒngqì 'courage') |
| Ptc | Particle (ma 'question particle', le 'completive verbal particle') |
| Prep | Preposition (cóng 'from', duìyú 'regarding') |
| V | Action Verb, transitive (mǎi 'buy', chī 'eat') |
| Vi | Action Verb, intransitive (kū 'cry', zuò 'sit') |
| Vaux | Auxiliary Verb (néng 'can', xiǎng 'would like to') |
| V-sep | Separable Verb (jiéhūn 'get married', shēngqì 'get angry') |
| Vs | State Verb, intransitive (hǎo 'good', guì 'expensive') |
| Vst | State Verb, transitive (xǐhuān 'like', zhīdào 'know') |
| Vs-attr | State Verb, attributive (zhǔyào 'primary', xiùzhēn 'mini-') |
| Vs-pred | State Verb, predicative (gòu 'enough', duō 'plenty') |
| Vp | Process Verb, intransitive (sǐ 'die', wán 'finish') |
| Vpt | Process Verb, transitive (pò (dòng) 'lit. break (hole) , liè (fèng) 'lit. crack (a crack)) |

**Notes:**

**Default values:** When no marking appears under a category, a default reading takes place, which has been built into the system by observing the commonest patterns of the highest frequency. A default value can be loosely understood as the most likely candidate. A default system results in using fewer symbols, which makes it easy on the eyes, reducing the amount of processing. Our default readings are as follows.

**Default transitivity.** When a verb is not marked, i.e. V, it's an action verb. An unmarked action verb, furthermore, is transitive. A state verb is marked as Vs, but if it's not further marked, it's intransitive. The same holds for process verbs, i.e. Vp is by default intransitive.

**Default position of adjectives.** Typical adjectives occur as predicates, e.g. 'This is great!' Therefore, unmarked Vs are predicative, and adjectives that cannot be predicates will be marked for this feature, e.g. zhǔyào 'primary' is an adjective but it cannot be a predicate, i.e. *Zhètiáo lù hěn zhǔyào. '*This road is very primary.' Therefore it is marked Vs-attr, meaning it can only be used attributively, i.e. zhǔyào dàolù 'primary road'. On the other hand, 'gòu' 'enough' in Chinese can only be used predicatively, not attributively, e.g. 'Shíjiān gòu' '*?Time is enough.', but not *gòu shíjiān 'enough time'. Therefore gòu is marked Vs-pred. Employing this new system of parts of speech guarantees good grammar!

**Default wordhood.** In English, words cannot be torn apart and be used separately, e.g. *mis- not – understand. Likewise in Chinese, e.g. *xǐbùhuān 'do not like'. However, there is a large group of words in Chinese that are exceptions to this probably universal rule and can be separated. They are called 'separable words', marked -sep in our new system of parts of speech. For example, shēngqì 'angry' is a word, but it is fine to say *shēng tā qì* 'angry at him'. Jiéhūn 'get married' is a word but it's fine to say *jiéguòhūn* 'been married before' or *jiéguò* sān cì *hūn* 'been married 3 times before'. There are at least a couple of hundred separable words in modern Chinese. Even native speakers have to learn that certain words can be separated. Thus, memorizing them is the only way to deal with them by learners, and our new system of parts of speech helps them along nicely. Go over the vocabulary lists in this series and look for the marking –sep.

Now, what motivates this severing of words? Ask Chinese gods, not your teachers! We only know a little about the syntactic circumstances under which they get separated. First and foremost, separable words are in most cases intransitive verbs, whether action, state or process. When these verbs are further associated with targets (nouns, conceptual objects), frequency (number of times), duration (for how long), occurrence (done, done away with) etc., separation takes pace and these associated elements are inserted in between. More examples are given below.

Wǒ jīnnián yǐjīng *kǎo*guò 20 cì *shì* le!! (I've taken 20 exams to date this year!)

Wǒ *dào*guò *qiàn* le; tā hái shēngqì! (I apologized, but he's still mad!)

*Fàng* sān tiān *jià*; dàjiā dōu zǒu le. (There will be a break of 3 days, and everyone has left.)

## Final Words

This is a very brief introduction to the modern Mandarin Chinese language, which is the standard world-wide. This introduction can only highlight the most salient properties of the language. Many other features of the language have been left out by design. For instance, nothing has been said about the patterns of word-formations in Chinese, and no presentation has been made of the unique written script of the language. Readers are advised to search on-line for resources relating to particular aspects of the language. For reading, please consult a highly readable best-seller in this regard, viz. Li, Charles and Sandra Thompson. 1982. Mandarin Chinese: a reference grammar. UC Los Angeles Press. (Authorised reprinting by Crane publishing Company, Taipei, Taiwan, still available as of October 2009).

# 各課重點　Highlights of Lessons

| Lessons | Topic & Themes | Learning Objectives | Grammar |
|---|---|---|---|
| **6** <br> Their School Is Up in the Mountains | Locations and Positions | 1. Learning to describe locations (e.g., near or far). <br> 2. Learning to talk about place in the vicinity of other places. <br> 3. Learning to make simple comments about the appearance of a place. | 1. Location Marker 在 zài <br> 2. Existential Sentence with 有 yǒu <br> 3. Softened Action V（一）V <br> 4. 不是 búshì Negation <br> 5. Location of an Activity |
| **7** <br> Going to KTV at 9 O'clock in the Morning | Time (Time-When and Time-Duration) | 1. Learning to tell and ask about time. <br> 2. Learning to describe an activity that takes place at a point in time (time-when) or during a certain frame (time-duration). <br> 3. Learning to make appointments with friends. <br> 4. Learning to talk about habitual activities. | 1. Time and Place of Events <br> 2. 從 cóng…到 dào… *from A to B* <br> 3. Progressive, On-going Actions 在 zài <br> 4. 每 měi *each and every* <br> 5. 可以 kěyǐ *permission* |
| **8** <br> Taking a Train to Tainan | Transportation | 1. Learning the names of different types of transportation and talking about getting to destinations. <br> 2. Learning to talk about some one's plans for their free time. <br> 3. Learning to make simple comparisons about various modes of transportation. <br> 4. Learning to explain likes and dislikes. | 1. Companionship with 跟 gēn <br> 2. Asking How with 怎麼 zěnme <br> 3. Implicit Comparison with 比較 bǐjiào <br> 4. 又 yòu…又 yòu *both A and B* <br> 5. Comparison with 比 bǐ |
| **9** <br> Where Will You Go for the Holidays? | Leisure | 1. Learning to use time expressions to describe events. <br> 2. Learning to discuss travel plans with friends. <br> 3. Learning to talk about hypothetical situations. <br> 4. Learning to give suggestions about leisure activities. | 1. Time-When vs. Time-Duration <br> 2. Time-Duration '*for a period of time*' <br> 3. …的時候 de shíhòu *when* <br> 4. 有時候 yǒu shíhòu…有時候 yǒu shíhò… *sometimes… sometimes…* <br> 5. Condition and Consequence with 要是 yàoshì…就 jiù… |
| **10** <br> The Fruit in Taiwan Tastes Really Good | The Appearance of People and Things | 1. Learning to give simple descriptions of someone's appearance. <br> 2. Learning to describe the color, smell, and taste of food. <br> 3. Learning to briefly explain and give reasons. <br> 4. Learning to describe tentative activities and changeable states. | 1. V V 看 kàn *to try and see* <br> 2. Intensification with Reduplicated State Verbs <br> 3. Clause as Modifiers of Nouns <br> 4. Change in Situation with Sentential 了 le <br> 5. Cause and Effect with 因為 yīnwèi…, 所以 suǒyǐ… |

# Parts of Speech in Chinese

## List of Parts of Speech in Chinese

| Symbols | Parts of speech | 八大詞類 | Examples |
|---------|-----------------|----------|----------|
| N | noun | 名詞 | 水、五、昨天、學校、他、幾 |
| V | verb | 動詞 | 吃、告訴、容易、快樂、知道、破 |
| Adv | adverb | 副詞 | 很、不、常、到處、也、就、難道 |
| Conj | conjunction | 連詞 | 和、跟、而且、雖然、因為 |
| Prep | preposition | 介詞 | 從、對、向、跟、在、給 |
| M | measure | 量詞 | 個、張、碗、次、頓、公尺 |
| Ptc | particle | 助詞 | 的、得、啊、嗎、完、掉、把、喂 |
| Det | determiner | 限定詞 | 這、那、某、每、哪 |

## Verb Classification

| Symbols | Classification | 動詞分類 | Examples |
|---------|----------------|----------|----------|
| V | transitive action verbs | 及物動作動詞 | 買、做、說 |
| Vi | intransitive action verbs | 不及物動作動詞 | 跑、坐、睡、笑 |
| V-sep | intransitive action verbs, separable | 不及物動作離合詞 | 唱歌、上網、打架 |
| Vs | intransitive state verbs | 不及物狀態動詞 | 冷、高、漂亮 |
| Vst | transitive state verbs | 及物狀態動詞 | 關心、喜歡、同意 |
| Vs-attr | intransitive state verbs, attributive only | 唯定不及物狀態動詞 | 野生、公共、新興 |
| Vs-pred | intransitive state verbs, predicative only | 唯謂不及物狀態動詞 | 夠、多、少 |
| Vs-sep | intransitive state verbs, separable | 不及物狀態離合詞 | 放心、幽默、生氣 |
| Vaux | auxiliary verbs | 助動詞 | 會、能、可以 |
| Vp | intransitive process verbs | 不及物變化動詞 | 破、感冒、壞、死 |
| Vpt | transitive process verbs | 及物變化動詞 | 忘記、變成、丟 |
| Vp-sep | intransitive process verbs, separable | 不及物變化離合詞 | 結婚、生病、畢業 |

## Default Values of the Symbols

| Symbols | Default values |
|---------|----------------|
| V | action, transitive |
| Vs | state, intransitive |
| Vp | process, intransitive |
| V-sep | separable, intransitive |

# 課堂用語 Classroom Phrases

**1** 上課了。
Shàngkè le.
Let's begin the class.

**2** 請打開書。
Qǐng dǎkāi shū.
Open your book.

**3** 請看第五頁。
Qǐng kàn dì wǔ yè.
Please see page 5.

**4** 我說，你們聽。
Wǒ shuō, nǐmen tīng.
I'll speak, you listen.

**5** 請跟我說。
Qǐng gēn wǒ shuō.
Please repeat after me.

**6** 請再說 / 念一次。
Qǐng zài shuō/niàn yí cì.
Please say it again.

**7** 請回答。
Qǐng huídá.
Please answer my question.

**8** 請問，這個字怎麼念 / 寫？
Qǐngwèn, zhè ge zì zěnme niàn/xiě?
How do you pronounce/spell this word?

**9** 對了！
Duì le!
Right! Correct!

**10** 不對。
Bú duì.
Wrong. Incorrect.

**11** 請念對話。
Qǐng niàn duìhuà.
Read the dialogue, please.

**12** 請看黑板。
Qǐng kàn hēibǎn.
Look at the board, please.

**13** 懂不懂？
Dǒng bù dǒng?
Do you understand?

**14** 懂了！
Dǒng le!
Yes, I/we understand.

**15** 有沒有問題？
Yǒu méi yǒu wèntí?
Any question?

**16** 很好！
Hěn hǎo!
Very good!

**17** 下課。
Xiàkè.
The class is over.

李明華

*Lǐ Mínghuá*

Li Ming-hua is from Taipei, Taiwan.
Male. Age 32. Single.

He works in a bank. He has worked in Vietnam for 6 months and is an acquaintance of Yue-mei Chen's father, who entrusted the responsibility of taking care of his daughter to Ming-hua. They met at the airport.

陳月美

*Chén Yuèměi*

Chen Yue-mei is from Hanoi, Vietnam.
Female. Age 22.

She traveled to Taiwan with her father's friend, Wang Kai-wen. They were picked up at the airport by Ming-hua, her father's Taiwanese acquaintance.
She is a student. Ru-yu and An-tong are her classmates.

白如玉

*Bái Rúyù*

Bai Ru-yu is from New York, USA.
Female. Age 21.

She is a student. Yue-mei and An-tong are her classmates.

馬安同

*Mǎ Āntóng*

Ma An-tong is from Tegucigalpa, Republic of Honduras.
Male. Age 22.

He is a student. Yue-mei and Ru-yu are his classmates.
He is Yi-jun's language exchange partner and Yi-jun is his best friend in Taiwan.

張怡君

*Zhāng Yíjūn*

Zhang Yi-jun is a Taiwanese college student.
Female. Age 20.

Her college is situated in a mountain in Hualien. She met An-tong on a trip. She is a language exchange partner of An-tong.

田中誠一

*Tiánzhōng Chéngyī*

Tianzhong Chengyi is from Tokyo, Japan.
Male. Age 30. Single.

He works in Taiwan as an expatriate of a Japanese motor company. Besides working, he is also learning Chinese in a language center. He is in the same class with Yue-mei, Ru-yu, and An-tong and he happens to be Li Ming-hua's client. Tianzhong's girlfriend is coming to Taiwan and he wants to show her around.

# 目 次 Contents

# Contents

# LESSON 6

## 第六課

# 他們學校在山上
## Their School Is Up in the Mountains

# 他們學校在山上

## Their School Is Up in the Mountains

**對話一 Dialogue 1**  06-01  06-A

| 安 | 同 | ：聽說怡君的學校很漂亮。 |
|---|---|---|
| 如 | 玉 | ：他們學校在哪裡？遠不遠？ |
| 安 | 同 | ：有一點遠。他們學校在花蓮的山上。 |
| 如 | 玉 | ：山上？那裡的風景一定很美。 |
| 安 | 同 | ：是的，他們學校前面有海，後面有山，<br>那裡真的是一個很漂亮的地方。 |
| 如 | 玉 | ：我想去看看。我們這個週末一起去吧！ |
| 安 | 同 | ：好啊！我現在要去學校附近的咖啡店<br>買咖啡。妳呢？ |
| 如 | 玉 | ：我去樓下找朋友，我們要一起去上課。 |

## 課文拼音 Text in Pinyin

Āntóng : Tīngshuō Yíjūn de xuéxiào hěn piàoliàng.

Rúyù : Tāmen xuéxiào zài nǎlǐ? Yuǎn bù yuǎn?

Āntóng : Yǒu yìdiǎn yuǎn. Tāmen xuéxiào zài Huālián de shānshàng.

Rúyù : Shānshàng? Nàlǐ de fēngjǐng yídìng hěn měi.

Āntóng : Shìde, tāmen xuéxiào qiánmiàn yǒu hǎi, hòumiàn yǒu shān. Nàlǐ
zhēnde shì yí ge hěn piàoliàng de dìfāng.

Rúyù : Wǒ xiǎng qù kànkàn. Wǒmen zhè ge zhōumò yìqǐ qù ba!

Āntóng : Hǎo a! Wǒ xiànzài yào qù xuéxiào fùjìn de kāfēi diàn mǎi kāfēi, nǐ ne?

Rúyù : Wǒ qù lóuxià zhǎo péngyǒu, wǒmen yào yìqǐ qù shàngkè.

## 課文英譯 Text in English

Antong : I heard Yijun's school is very beautiful.

Ruyu : Where is her school? Is it far?

Antong : It is a bit far. Her school is up in the mountains in Hualien.

Ruyu : Up in the mountains? The scenery there must be very beautiful.

Antong : Yes. In front of their school is the ocean and behind it there are mountains.
It is really a beautiful place.

Ruyu : I'd like to go see. Let's go together this weekend.

Antong : Okay. I am going to go to a café near the school now to buy some coffee.
How about you?

Ruyu : I am going to go downstairs to meet a friend. We are going to go to class together.

## 生詞一 Vocabulary 1  06-02

### Vocabulary

| 1 | 他們 | tāmen | ㄊㄚ ㄇㄣ | (N) | they (used for people only) |
|---|------|-------|---------|-----|------------------------------|
| 2 | 學校 | xuéxiào | ㄒㄩㄝ ㄒㄧㄠ | (N) | school |
| 3 | 在 | zài | ㄗㄞ | (Vst) | to be located at |

3

| 4 | 山上 | shānshàng | ㄕㄢ ㄕㄤˋ | (N) | on a mountain, in the mountains |
| 5 | 哪裡 | nǎlǐ | ㄋㄚˇ ㄌㄧˇ | (N) | where |
| 6 | 遠 | yuǎn | ㄩㄢˇ | (Vs) | far |
| 7 | 那裡 | nàlǐ | ㄋㄚˋ ㄌㄧˇ | (N) | that place, there |
| 8 | 風景 | fēngjǐng | ㄈㄥ ㄐㄧㄥˇ | (N) | scenery, landscape |
| 9 | 美 | měi | ㄇㄟˇ | (Vs) | beautiful |
| 10 | 前面 | qiánmiàn | ㄑㄧㄢˊ ㄇㄧㄢˋ | (N) | front |
| 11 | 海 | hǎi | ㄏㄞˇ | (N) | ocean |
| 12 | 後面 | hòumiàn | ㄏㄡˋ ㄇㄧㄢˋ | (N) | back |
| 13 | 山 | shān | ㄕㄢ | (N) | mountain |
| 14 | 真的 | zhēnde | ㄓㄣ ㄉㄜ | (Adv) | really, truly |
| 15 | 地方 | dìfāng | ㄉㄧˋ ㄈㄤ | (N) | place |
| 16 | 現在 | xiànzài | ㄒㄧㄢˋ ㄗㄞˋ | (N) | now |
| 17 | 附近 | fùjìn | ㄈㄨˋ ㄐㄧㄣˋ | (N) | vicinity, near |
| 18 | 樓下 | lóuxià | ㄌㄡˊ ㄒㄧㄚˋ | (N) | downstairs |
| 19 | 找 | zhǎo | ㄓㄠˇ | (V) | to meet, to see |
| 20 | 朋友 | péngyǒu | ㄆㄥˊ ㄧㄡˇ | (N) | friend |
| 21 | 上課 | shàngkè | ㄕㄤˋ ㄎㄜˋ | (V-sep) | to go to class |

## Names

| 22 | 花蓮 | Huālián | ㄏㄨㄚ ㄌㄧㄢˊ | | Hualien, name of a city on the eastern coast of Taiwan |

## Phrases

| 23 | 聽說 | tīngshuō | ㄊㄧㄥ ㄕㄨㄛ | | hear that |

對話二 Dialogue **2**     06-03     06-B

| | | |
|---|---|---|
| 怡 | 君 | ：歡迎你們來。 |
| 安 | 同 | ：你們學校真遠！ |
| 怡 | 君 | ：是啊，不是很近，有一點不方便。 |
| 如 | 玉 | ：這裡的學生在哪裡買東西？ |
| 怡 | 君 | ：在學校外面。學校裡面沒有商店。 |
| 安 | 同 | ：吃飯呢？學校裡面有沒有餐廳？ |
| 怡 | 君 | ：有，餐廳在學生宿舍的一樓。 |
| 安 | 同 | ：前面這棟大樓很漂亮。 |
| 怡 | 君 | ：這是圖書館，旁邊的那棟大樓是教室，<br>圖書館後面有游泳池。 |

## 課文拼音 Text in Pinyin

Yíjūn : Huānyíng nǐmen lái.

Āntóng : Nǐmen xuéxiào zhēn yuǎn!

Yíjūn : Shì a, búshì hěn jìn, yǒu yìdiǎn bù fāngbiàn.

Rúyù : Zhèlǐ de xuéshēng zài nǎlǐ mǎi dōngxi?

Yíjūn : Zài xuéxiào wàimiàn. Xuéxiào lǐmiàn méi yǒu shāngdiàn.

Āntóng : Chīfàn ne? Xuéxiào lǐmiàn yǒu méi yǒu cāntīng?

Yíjūn : Yǒu, cāntīng zài xuéshēng sùshè de yì lóu.

Āntóng : Qiánmiàn zhè dòng dàlóu hěn piàoliàng.

Yíjūn : Zhè shì túshūguǎn, pángbiān de nà dòng dàlóu shì jiàoshì, túshūguǎn hòumiàn yǒu yóuyǒngchí.

## 課文英譯 Text in English

Yijun : Welcome.

Antong : Your school is really far.

Yijun : Yes. It's not close. It's a little inconvenient.

Ruyu : Where do the students here buy things?

Yijun : Outside of the school. There are no shops on campus.

Antong : How about eating? Do you have restaurants on campus?

Yijun : Yes. The restaurants are located on the first floor of the student dorm.

Antong : That building in front of us is pretty.

Yijun : This is the library. The building next to it are the classrooms. Behind the library, there is a swimming pool.

## 生詞二 Vocabulary   🎧 06-04

### Vocabulary

| | | | | | |
|---|---|---|---|---|---|
| 1 | 近 | jìn | ㄐㄧㄣˋ | (Vs) | near |
| 2 | 方便 | fāngbiàn | ㄈㄤ ㄅㄧㄢˋ | (Vs) | convenient |
| 3 | 這裡 | zhèlǐ | ㄓㄜˋ ㄌㄧˇ | (N) | here, this place |

| 4 | 學生 | xuéshēng | ㄒㄩㄝˊ ㄕㄥ | (N) | student |
| 5 | 在 | zài | ㄗㄞˋ | (Prep) | at |
| 6 | 東西 | dōngxi | ㄉㄨㄥ ㄒㄧ˙ | (N) | things, stuff |
| 7 | 外面 | wàimiàn | ㄨㄞˋ ㄇㄧㄢˋ | (N) | outside |
| 8 | 裡面 | lǐmiàn | ㄌㄧˇ ㄇㄧㄢˋ | (N) | inside |
| 9 | 商店 | shāngdiàn | ㄕㄤ ㄉㄧㄢˋ | (N) | store, shop |
| 10 | 吃飯 | chīfàn | ㄔ ㄈㄢˋ | (V-sep) | to have a meal |
| 11 | 宿舍 | sùshè | ㄙㄨˋ ㄕㄜˋ | (N) | dormitory |
| 12 | 樓 | lóu | ㄌㄡˊ | (N) | a storey, a floor |
| 13 | 棟 | dòng | ㄉㄨㄥˋ | (M) | measure word for buildings |
| 14 | 大樓 | dàlóu | ㄉㄚˋ ㄌㄡˊ | (N) | a multi-storey building |
| 15 | 圖書館 | túshūguǎn | ㄊㄨˊ ㄕㄨ ㄍㄨㄢˇ | (N) | library |
| 16 | 旁邊 | pángbiān | ㄆㄤˊ ㄅㄧㄢ | (N) | (by the) side, next to |
| 17 | 教室 | jiàoshì | ㄐㄧㄠˋ ㄕˋ | (N) | classroom |
| 18 | 游泳池 | yóuyǒngchí | ㄧㄡˊ ㄩㄥˇ ㄔˊ | (N) | swimming pool |

## 文法 Grammar

### I. Locative Marker 在 zài   06-05

 拼音、英譯 p.18

**Function:** 在 *zài* introduces the location of someone or something.

| 我在臺灣。 | 他們學校在花蓮。 | 餐廳在宿舍的一樓。 |

**Structures:** The primary structure is Noun + 在 + Location. There are three types of location as shown below:

1. **Type A:**

| Place Words |
| --- |
| 臺北、花蓮、臺灣… |
| 學校、餐廳、宿舍… |

(1) 我們學校在臺北。
(2) 我爸爸早上在學校。

2. **Type B:**

| Localizers | | Suffix |
| --- | --- | --- |
| 上 | top | |
| 下 | down | |
| 前 | front | |
| 後 | back | 面 or 邊 |
| 裡 | inside | |
| 外 | outside | |
| 旁邊 next to | | |
| 附近 nearby | | |

(1) 他在外面。
(2) 圖書館在後面。

3. **Type C:**

| Noun | （的） | Location Type B | |
| --- | --- | --- | --- |
| | | 上 | |
| | | 下 | |
| | | 前 | |
| | | 後 | 面 or 邊 |
| | | 裡 | |
| | | 外 | |
| | | 旁邊 | |
| | | 附近 | |

(1) 我在宿舍裡面。
(2) 那家店在你家附近嗎？
(3) 咖啡店在宿舍的旁邊，不在裡面。
(4) 游泳池在圖書館的後面，不在前面。
(5) 他和朋友在圖書館後面的咖啡店。

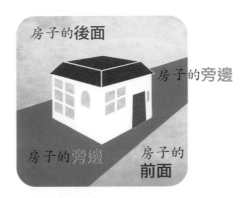

## Usage:

1. When the noun after 在 *zài* is a common noun, a locative word has to be added after the common noun to turn it into a place name. For example, in order to express "He is in the house", you cannot say *他在房子 Tā zài fángzi; rather, you need to say 他在房子裡面。Tā zài fángzi lǐmiàn. (房子裡面 is Type C with the 的 omitted.)

2. When the noun after 在 *zài* is a proper name, a locative word is not allowed or necessary. For example, in order to express "He is in Taiwan.", one says 他在臺灣。Tā zài Táiwān, but not *他在臺灣裡面。 Tā zài Táiwān lǐmiàn. On the other hand, in order to express "He is in school", one can say either 他在學校。Tā zài xuéxiào, or 他在學校裡面。Tā zài xuéxiào lǐmiàn. The addition of the locative word (裡面 *lǐmiàn*, in this case) makes the location more explicit.

3. The locative word 裡面 *lǐmiàn* is a special case. Sometimes, it can be omitted. For example, 他在圖書館看書。Tā zài túshūguǎn kànshū means "He's reading in the library". There is no 裡面 *lǐmiàn* in the sentence, but the sentence still means inside the library. However, when the intended meaning is not "inside", then a locative word is **required**. For example, in order to express "He is reading outside the library", one has to say 他在圖書館外面看書。Tā zài túshūguǎn wàimiàn kànshū.

4. Notice that the reference point is placed first and the locative word is placed after it. For example, 房子的前面 *fángzi de qiánmiàn* "in front of the house" is different from 前面的房子 *qiánmiàn de fángzi* "the house in front". (The former is Type C, but the latter is modifier + noun.)

（學校）附近的咖啡店　　　咖啡店的附近

5. Abbreviations of locative phrases without 的 are common. For example, "downstairs" is 樓下 *lóuxià*, not *樓的下面 *lóu de xiàmiàn*; "on the floor" is 地上 *dìshàng*, not * 地的上面 *dì de shàngmiàn*.

6. When the 的 is omitted, the suffix 面 *miàn* in 裡面 *lǐmiàn*, 外面 *wàimiàn*, 上面 *shàngmiàn*, etc, can be omitted. For example, 房子的裡面 *fángzi de lǐmiàn* "inside the house" is often just 房子裡 *fángzi lǐ* and 杯子上面 *bēizi shàngmiàn* "on the cup" is shortened to 杯子上 *bēizi shàng*.

---

**練習 Exercise**

**1. Use the following expressions to describe the four pictures below.**

| 餐廳 | 商店 | 咖啡店 | 大樓 | 圖書館 | 游泳池 |
|------|------|--------|------|--------|--------|
| 前面 | 後面 | 裡面 | 外面 | 旁邊 | 附近 |

咖啡店（的）裡面

## 練習 Exercise

### 2. 他在哪裡？Where is he? Give answers based on the pictures.

### 3. Fill in the blanks below based on the pictures.

大樓的前面、前面的大樓、餐廳後面、後面的（那家）餐廳

_____ 很美。

我在 _____。

_____ 很便宜。

他在 _____。

## 練習 Exercise

Combine the clauses.

**1** 他在咖啡店，那家咖啡店在陽明山（Yangming Mountain）山上。
→ <u>他在陽明山山上的（那家）咖啡店。</u>

**2** 他在圖書館，那個圖書館在他家附近。
→ _____ 。

**3** 他姐姐在那棟大樓裡面，那棟大樓在學校後面。
→ _____ 。

**4** 我和我朋友在一家咖啡店，那家咖啡店在學校餐廳（的）樓上。
→ _____ 。

## II. Existential Sentences with 有 yǒu  06-06

**Function:** The existential verb 有 *yǒu* expresses the existence of somebody or something at some location.

**1** 那棟大樓（的）前面有很多人。
**2** 我家附近有圖書館。
**3** 山上有兩家很有名的咖啡店。
**4** 樓下有一家商店。

**Structures:** The existential structure is: Location ＋ 有 ＋ Noun. The internal structures of location here are the same as the location introduced above in the locative sentences.

**Negation:** The negation for existential sentences is 沒有 *méi yǒu*.

**1** 他家附近沒有游泳池。
**2** 教室裡面沒有學生。
**3** 那棟大樓的後面沒有餐廳。

✏️ **Questions:**

**❶** 你家附近有海嗎？

**❷** 學校（的）後面有沒有好吃的牛肉麵店？

**Usage:**

1. The object in existential sentences is usually indefinite, i.e., the identification of the object is not readily certain or familiar to the speaker.
   Note also that existential sentences and locative sentences are just the reverse in sequence, e.g., 樓下有圖書館 vs. 圖書館在樓下。
   Lóuxià yǒu túshūguǎn. vs. Túshūguǎn zài lóuxià.
   "Downstairs there is a library." vs. "The library is downstairs."

2. In 我有一支手機 Wǒ yǒu yì zhī shǒujī "I have a cellphone", the verb 有 is possessive and transitive and in 房子裡面有一支手機 Fángzi lǐmiàn yǒu yì zhī shǒujī "There is a cellphone in the house", the verb 有 is existential and intransitive. The possessive 有 is always transitive, while the existential 有 is always intransitive.

**練習 Exercise**

Rearrange the order of the following characters to form acceptable sentences.

**❶** 有　很多漂亮的房子　山上
　　①　　　②　　　　　③　　　→＿＿＿＿＿＿＿＿＿＿＿。

**❷** 樓下　咖啡店　嗎　有
　　①　　②　　③　④　　→＿＿＿＿＿＿＿＿＿＿？

**❸** 裡面　沒有　他們學校　游泳池
　　①　　②　　　③　　　　④　　→＿＿＿＿＿＿＿＿＿＿。

**❹** 的　教室　外面　兩個美國人　有
　　①　②　　③　　　④　　　⑤　→＿＿＿＿＿＿＿＿＿＿。

## III. Softened Action V（一）V  06-07

拼音、英譯 p.19

**Function:** Verb reduplication suggests "reduced quantity". It also suggests that the action is easy to accomplish. When what is expressed is a request/command, verb reduplication softens the tone of the statement and the hearer finds the request/command more moderate.

**❶** 他們學校很漂亮，我想去看（一）看。

**❷** 我想學中文，請教教我。

**❸** A：我們今天晚上去哪裡吃飯？
　　B：我想（一）想。

**❹** A：你週末做什麼？
　　B：在家看看書、喝喝咖啡、上上網，也去學校打打籃球。

### Structures:

 **Questions:** There are two ways to form verb reduplication in interrogatives.

1. Tag question:
   **(1)** 請幫幫我，好不好？
   **(2)** 請你教教我，可以嗎？

2. With an auxiliary verb:
   **(1)** 現在外面很熱，你要不要在家看看書？
   **(2)** 我不會做甜點，你可不可以教教我？

### Usage:

1. Not every verb can be reduplicated. Mainly action verbs can go undergo verb repetition. Of the verbs we've learned so far, the verbs that can be reduplicated include 看 *kàn*, 吃 *chī*, 喝 *hē*, 想 *xiǎng*, 做 *zuò*, 打 *dǎ*, 找 *zhǎo*, 買 *mǎi*, 教 *jiāo*, and 幫 *bāng*.

2. Verb reduplication is mostly used in speech for requests and suggestions. Most reduplicated verbs are monosyllabic. When the verb takes an object, only the verb gets reduplicated, not the object. For example, 上網 *shàngwǎng* 'go online' is changed to 上上網 *shàngshàng wǎng*; 做飯 *zuòfàn* 'cook' is changed to 做做飯 *zuòzuòfàn*.

1. Reduplicate the following verbs.

❶ 做飯 → 做做飯　　❷ 喝茶 → _____

❸ 吃甜點 → _____　　❹ 打網球 → _____

❺ 踢足球 → _____　　❻ 游泳 → _____

❼ 看電影 → _____　　❽ 照相 → _____

2. Fill in the blanks with correctly reduplicated verbs plus any object needed.

看、吃、喝、想、做、打、找、買、教、幫

❶ 那個電影很好看，我想去 _____。

❷ 我不會做飯，請你 _____。

❸ 我想學照相，能不能請你 _____ ？

❹ 週末我喜歡到外面 _____。

❺ A：那支手機很貴，你要買嗎？

　　B：_____。

## IV. 不是 búshì　Negation　🎧 06-08　拼音、英譯 p.20

**Function:** 不是 *búshì* is not a regular negator. It negates what has been stated or assumed, i.e., "it is not true that...," for example,

❶ 明華覺得那支手機很貴。我覺得不是很貴。

❷ 他不是點大碗的牛肉麵。他點小碗的。

❸ 餐廳不是在學校裡面。餐廳在學校外面。

**Structures:** The 不是 *búshì* negation can occur in either positive or negative sentences, e.g.,

**❶** 他們不是在樓下喝咖啡。他們在樓下買書。

**❷** 我不是不來，我週末來。

**❸** 我不是不喜歡吃牛肉麵，可是這家的牛肉麵太辣了。

**Usage:** We have already covered 不 *bù* negation and 沒 *méi* negation. 不是 *búshì* negation is quite different. It negates what has been said or claimed, "It is not the case that...".

他不要買包子。**vs.** 他不是要買包子，他要買臭豆腐。

---

**練習 Exercise**

Please use the phrase 不是 to complete the following conversation.

**❶** A：你朋友的家在三樓，對嗎？

　　B：＿＿＿＿＿＿＿＿＿＿，他家在四樓。

**❷** A：你們覺得這家店的甜點好吃嗎？

　　B：我妹妹覺得很好吃，可是我覺得＿＿＿＿＿＿＿＿。

**❸** A：很多人都說你做飯做得很好。

　　B：我做得＿＿＿＿＿＿＿＿，我媽媽做得很好。

**❹** A：你的照片不多，你不喜歡照相嗎？

　　B：＿＿＿＿＿＿＿＿，我不常照相，所以我的照片不多。

**❺** A：你晚上不想去他家聽音樂嗎？

　　B：＿＿＿＿＿＿＿＿，我晚上要和老闆吃飯。

## V. Location of an Activity  🎧 06-09

拼音、英譯 p.21

**Function:** 在 *zài* 'at' and 到 *dào* 'go to', are often used to introduce the location where an activity takes place.

**❶** 我爸爸在家做飯。

**❷** 他和他朋友到七樓的教室上網。

**❸** 我們老師常到學校附近的咖啡店喝咖啡。

**❹** 我們很喜歡在這家餐廳吃牛肉麵。

**Structures:** The location usually follows one of the these words: 在 *zài* 'at', 到 *dào* 'go to'. The action expression follows the location phrase.

🖊 **Negation:** The negation marker 不 *bú* is placed before 在 *zài* / 到 *dào*, rather than before the verb.

**❶** 他們今天不在家吃晚飯。

**❷** 他現在不在宿舍看書。

**❸** 很多學生不在學校裡面的咖啡店買咖啡。

🖊 **Questions:**

**❶** 你們在哪裡打籃球？

**❷** 你妹妹到這家商店買甜點嗎？

**Usage:**

1. Note the word order. The location comes before the main verb. That is, the " 在 *zài* / 到 *dào* + PLACE" phrase appears before the verb phrase as do all prepositional phrases. You do not say * 他學中文在家 Tā xué Zhōngwén zài jiā; rather you say 他在家學中文。Tā zài jiā xué Zhōngwén. 'He studies Chinese at home'.

2. The negation is placed before the preposition rather than the main verb, e.g., 他 不在家上網。Tā bú zài jiā shàngwǎng. 'He doesn't use the internet at home.'

## 練習 Exercise

Tell stories based on the pictures below.

姐姐在家裡
做飯。

---

### 語法例句拼音與英譯
### Grammar Examples in Pinyin and English

## I. Locative Marker 在 zài

**Function:**

Wǒ zài Táiwān.
Tāmen xuéxiào zài Huālián.
Cāntīng zài sùshè de yì lóu.

**Function:**

I am in Taiwan.
Their school is in Hualien.
The restaurant is on the first floor of the dormitory.

**Structures:**

1. **Type A:**
   (1) Wǒmen xuéxiào zài Táiběi.
   (2) Wǒ bàba zǎoshàng zài xuéxiào.

2. **Type B:**
   (1) Tā zài wàimiàn.
   (2) Túshūguǎn zài hòumiàn.

3. **Type C:**
   (1) Wǒ zài sùshè lǐmiàn.
   (2) Nà jiā diàn zài nǐ jiā fùjìn ma?
   (3) Kāfēi diàn zài sùshè de pángbiān, bú zài lǐmiàn.
   (4) Yóuyǒngchí zài túshūguǎn de hòumiàn, bú zài qiánmiàn.
   (5) Tā hàn péngyǒu zài túshūguǎn hòumiàn de kāfēidiàn.

**Structures:**

1. **Type A:**
   (1) Our school is in Taipei.
   (2) My dad is at school in the mornings.

2. **Type B:**
   (1) He is outside.
   (2) The library is in the back.

3. **Type C:**
   (1) I am in the dormintory.
   (2) Is that store near your house?
   (3) The coffee shop is next to the dorm, not inside.
   (4) The swimming pool is behind the library, not in front.
   (5) He and his friend are at the coffee shop behind the library.

## II. Existential Sentences with 有 yǒu

### Function:.

1 Nà dòng dàlóu (de) qiánmiàn yǒu hěn duō rén.
2 Wǒ jiā fùjìn yǒu túshūguǎn.
3 Shānshàng yǒu liǎng jiā hěn yǒumíng de kāfēi diàn.
4 Lóuxià yǒu yì jiā shāngdiàn.

### Function:.

1 There are many people in front of that building.
2 There is a library near my home.
3 There are two famous coffee shops on the mountain.
4 There is a shop downstairs.

### Structures:

🖊 **Negation:**

1 Tā jiā fùjìn méi yǒu yóuyǒngchí.
2 Jiàoshì lǐmiàn méi yǒu xuéshēng.
3 Nà dòng dàlóu de hòumiàn méi yǒu cāntīng.

🖊 **Questions:**

1 Nǐ jiā fùjìn yǒu hǎi ma?
2 Xuéxiào (de) hòumiàn yǒu méi yǒu hǎochī de niúròu miàn diàn?

### Structures:

🖊 **Negation:**

1 There is no swimming pool near his home.
2 There is no student in the classroom.
3 There is no restaurant behind that building.

🖊 **Questions:**

1 Is there ocean near your house?
2 Is there a good beef noodle shop behind the school?

## III. Softened Action V（一）V

### Function:

1 Tāmen xuéxiào hěn piàoliàng, wǒ xiǎng qù kàn (yí) kàn.
2 Wǒ xiǎng xué Zhōngwén, qǐng jiāojiāo wǒ.
3 A: Wǒmen jīntiān wǎnshàng qù nǎlǐ chīfàn?
   B: Wǒ xiǎng (yì) xiǎng.
4 A: Nǐ zhōumò zuò shénme?
   B: Zài jiā kànkàn shū, hēhē kāfēi, shàngshàngwǎng, yě qù xuéxiào dǎdǎ lánqiú.

### Function:

1 Their school is pretty. I'd like to take a look.
2 I'd like to study Chinese. Please teach me.
3 A: Where are we going to go for dinner tonight?
   B: Let me think.
4 A: What do you do on weekends?
   B: I stay home and do some reading, have some coffee, and do some surfing on the internet. I also go to school and play some basketball.

## Structures:

### 🖊 Questions:

1. Tag question:
   **(1)** Qǐng bāngbāng wǒ, hǎo bù hǎo?
   **(2)** Qǐng nǐ jiāojiāo wǒ, kěyǐ ma?

2. With an auxiliary verb:
   **(1)** Xiànzài wàimiàn hěn rè, nǐ yào bú yào zài jiā kànkàn shū?
   **(2)** Wǒ bú huì zuò tiándiǎn, nǐ kě bù kěyǐ jiāojiāo wǒ?

## IV. 不是 búshì  Negation

### Function:

❶ Mínghuá juéde nà zhī shǒujī hěn guì. Wǒ juéde búshì hěn guì.

❷ Tā búshì diǎn dà wǎn de niúròu miàn. Tā diǎn xiǎo wǎn de.

❸ Cāntīng búshì zài xuéxiào lǐmiàn. Cāntīng zài xuéxiào wàimiàn.

### Structures:

❶ Tāmen búshì zài lóuxià hē kāfēi. Tāmen zài lóuxià mǎi shū.

❷ Wǒ búshì bù lái, wǒ zhōumò lái.

❸ Wǒ búshì bù xǐhuān chī niúròu miàn, kěshì zhè jiā de niúròu miàn tài là le.

### Usage:

Tā bú yào mǎi bāozi vs. Tā búshì yào mǎi bāozi, tā yào mǎi chòudòufǔ.

## Structures:

### 🖊 Questions:

1   Tag question:
   **(1)** Please help me, OK?
   **(2)** Please teach me, OK?

2. With an auxiliary verb:
   **(1)** It is hot outside now. Would you like to do some reading at home?
   **(2)** I don't know how to make desserts. Could you teach me?

### Function:

❶ Minghua feels that cell phone is expensive. I think it's not all that expensive.

❷ He didn't order a large bowl of beef noodles. He ordered a small one.

❸ The restaurant isn't on campus. The restaurant is off campus.

### Structures:

❶ It's not the case that they are drinking coffee downstairs. They are buying books downstairs.

❷ I am not not coming. I am coming on the weekend.

❸ It's not that I don't like beef noodles; rather, it's that this shop's beef noodles are too spicy.

### Usage:

He isn't buying baozi. vs. It's not that he's buying baozi. He's buying stinky tofu.

## V. Location of an Activity

### Function:

① Wǒ bàba zài jiā zuòfàn.
② Tā hàn tā péngyǒu dào qī lóu de jiàoshì shàngwǎng.
③ Wǒmen lǎoshī cháng dào xuéxiào fùjìn de kāfēi diàn hē kāfēi.
④ Wǒmen hěn xǐhuān zài zhè jiā cāntīng chī niúròu miàn.

### Structures:

🖊 **Negation:**

① Tāmen jīntiān bú zài jiā chī wǎnfàn.

② Tā xiànzài bú zài sùshè kànshū.

③ Hěn duō xuéshēng bú zài xuéxiào lǐmiàn de kāfēi diàn mǎi kāfēi.

🖊 **Questions:**

① Nǐmen zài nǎlǐ dǎ lánqiú?
② Nǐ mèimei dào zhè jiā shāngdiàn mǎi tiándiǎn ma?

### Function:

① My dad is cooking at home.
② He and his friends went to the classroom on the seventh floor to use the internet.
③ Our teacher often goes to a coffee shop near to the school to drink coffee.
④ We love to eat beef noodles in this restaurant.

### Structures:

🖊 **Negation:**

① They aren't eating dinner at home today.
② He is not studying in the dormitory now.
③ Many students do not buy coffee at the coffee shop in the school.

🖊 **Questions:**

① Where do you play basketball?
② Does your sister come to this shop to buy desserts?

## Classroom Activities

### I. Where Are They?

**Goal:** Learning to describe someone's location.

**Task 1:** Look at the picture below, and write down where each person is.

**Task 2:** Write your name anywhere on the picture, then take a look at the picture of the person next to you and tell the class where s/he is. Listen to all the students and write down where everyone is. Have your teacher check to see if you are correct.

**Write down where they are :**

怡君在 _____ （的）_____ （教室、裡面）

如玉

安同

月美

明華

田中

## II. Tell Us about the Place You Live

**Goal:** Learning to make simple comments about the location and the appearance of a place.

**Task:** You would like to invite a classmate to your house (you live near the school). Tell him where your house is, what is nearby, what you can do at home or in the neighborhood, and what you can eat nearby.

| | 問題 Questions | 使用生詞 Words to use | 同學 1 Classmate 1 | 同學 2 Classmate 2 |
|---|---|---|---|---|
| 1 | 你家在哪裡？ | | | |

| 2 | 你家附近怎麼樣？ | 風景美嗎？ | | |
|---|---|---|---|---|
| 3 | 你家附近有什麼？ | 商店、學校、餐廳、大樓、房子、游泳池、圖書館、咖啡店、山、海 | | |
| 4 | 你喜歡在家裡做什麼？ | 吃飯、喝咖啡、看書 | | |
| 5 | 你常在家附近做什麼？ | 吃飯、看電影、打球、買東西 | | |

## III. I Want to Know About Your School

**Goal:** Learning to talk about your school in your country.

**Task:** Pair up with a partner and ask about his/her school. You can use the following questions to help you obtain information. When you are done, report your findings to the class.

(List your answers.)

**❶** 你的學校裡有什麼？（教室、商店、咖啡店、餐廳、圖書館、游泳池、學生宿舍）

_____

**❷** 你的學校風景怎麼樣？美不美？學校附近呢？

_____

**❸** 你的學校附近有什麼？（山、海、商店、餐廳）

_____

**❹** 你常在學校附近做什麼？（喝咖啡、打球、游泳、吃飯、看電影、上網、看書）

_____

**文化 Bits of Chinese Culture**

# Taboos with the Number " 四 " *sì* and Lucky Numbers " 六 " *liù* and " 八 " *bā*

Why is the number 4 *sì* shunned by Taiwanese? And why do they especially like the numbers 6 *liù* and 8 *bā*? This has everything to do with the Chinese culture of homophones. Since the number 4 *sì* sounds almost the same as the word " 死 " *sǐ* "death," it is disliked by most Chinese. That is also the reason why some hospitals do not have a fourth floor, and some people avoid buying houses with a number 4 *sì* in the mailing address. Therefore, if a house were located on the "4th Floor, No. 4, Zhongshan Road, Section 4," this house is very likely to be cheaper than the surrounding houses. On the other hand, since the number 6 *liù* sounds like the word " 祿 *lù*", meaning the salary of a government official (in ancient China), and the number 8 *bā* sounds like the word " 發 *fā*", meaning "to strike it rich", they are popular with the Chinese.

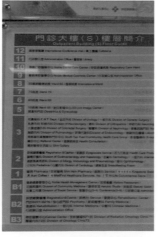

▲ Some hospitals in Taiwan don't have 4th floors

▲ People and businesses like certain lucky numbers
照片提供：台灣大車隊

## Birth Rate vs. Private Schools

Running a school is difficult, be it private or public, but this is especially so for private schools. As low birth rate exacerbates, keeping the school in operation is becoming an even harder mission. As more and more people choose to refrain from parenthood, fewer and fewer children are being born each year. According to statistics from the Ministry of Interior, there were 305,000 new borns in 2000. This number dropped to 167,000 in 2010, though with a slight comeback in 2012 at 229,000 new borns. Fewer children mean fewer students enrolled in schools. Many departments and schools are being confronted with the problem of shutting down or merging with other schools; and this phenomenon is mostly seen in private schools.

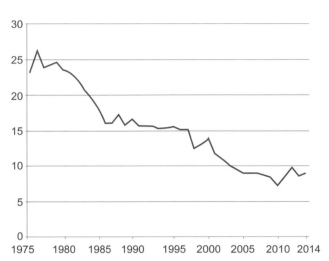

▲ Birth rate chart for the last 30 years
資料來源：內政部戶部司

▲ Students in private schools
《聯合報》王長鼎、廖珮妤 攝影

## Introduction to Chinese Characters
### The Six Categories of Chinese Characters

Chinese characters can be divided into six categories known as the Six Writings " 六書 " *liùshū*.

1. **Pictograms**（象形）: Characters in this category are idealized shapes of objects. Examples include sun " 日 ," moon " 月 ," mountain " 山 ," river " 川 ," water " 水 ," fire " 火 ," cow " 牛 ," sheep " 羊 ," child " 子."

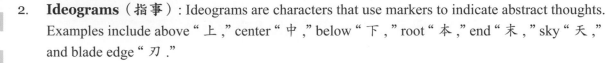

2. **Ideograms**（指事）: Ideograms are characters that use markers to indicate abstract thoughts. Examples include above "上," center "中," below "下," root "本," end "末," sky "天," and blade edge "刃."

3. **Compound ideographs**（會意）: These characters use a combination of two or more characters to form a new character with a new meaning. Examples include bright "明"（from sun "日" and moon "月"）, cut down "伐"（person "人" + spear "戈"）, imprison "囚"（enclose "口" + person "人"）, trust "信"（person "人" + speech "言"）, rest "休"（person "人" + tree "木"）, look "看"（hand "手" + eye "目"）.

4. **Phono-semantic compounds**（形聲）: These characters are made up of a phonetic component and a semantic component. Examples include sunny "晴"（the phonetic of blue "青" + the semantic of sun "日"）, clear "清"（the phonetic of blue "青" + the semantic of water "水," which came to mean "clear water."）

5. **Derivative cognates**（轉注）: This category consists primarily of character pairs of different shapes with the same meaning or similar meanings derived in different places and at different times. For example, the characters "考" and "老" both mean "old age."

6. **Phonetic loans**（假借）: Some concepts originally could be said but did not have any characters to represent them, so characters with the same or similar pronunciation were borrowed. For example, the character "西," which originally meant birds resting on a tree, was borrowed to mean "west."

## Self-Assessment Checklist

I can describe a location (e.g., near or far) or position.

20%    40%    60%    80%    100%

I can talk about a place closely around one's work and life.

20%    40%    60%    80%    100%

I can make simple comments about the appearance of a place.

20%    40%    60%    80%    100%

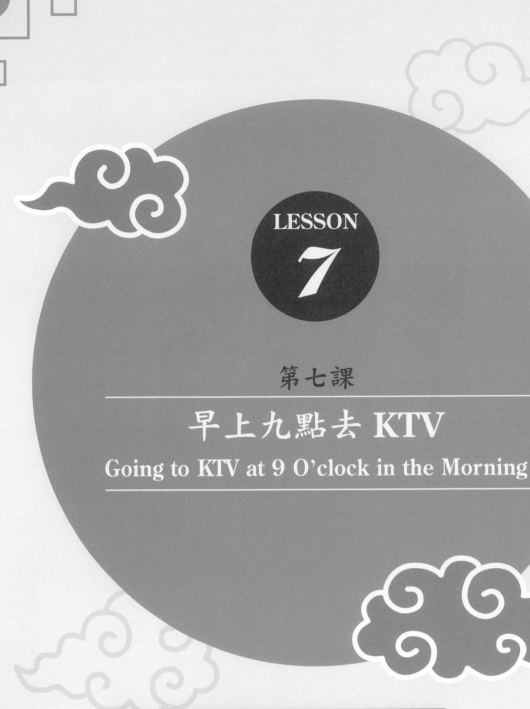

第七課

# 早上九點去 KTV
## Going to KTV at 9 O'clock in the Morning

**學習目標 Learning Objectives**

**Topic:** 時間（時點、時段）**Time**
**(Time-When and Time-Duration)**

- Learning to tell and ask about time.
- Learning to describe an activity that takes place at a point in time (time-when) or during a certain frame (time-duration).
- Learning to make appointments with friends.
- Learning to talk about habitual activities.

# 早上九點去 KTV

## Going to KTV at 9 O'clock in the Morning

**對話一 Dialogue 1**　　🎧 07-01　　AR 07-A

| 安 | 同 | ：月美，妳要去哪裡？ |
|---|---|---|
| 月 | 美 | ：去 KTV 唱歌。我和朋友九點二十分在大安 KTV 見面。 |
| 安 | 同 | ：早上九點去 KTV？為什麼？ |
| 月 | 美 | ：從早上七點到中午十二點，最便宜。要不要一起去？ |
| 安 | 同 | ：我想去，可是我得去銀行。下次吧！ |
| 月 | 美 | ：好啊，下次你一定要來，我想聽你唱歌。 |
| 安 | 同 | ：沒問題。對了，什麼時候有空一起吃飯？ |
| 月 | 美 | ：後天我有空，你呢？ |
| 安 | 同 | ：我也有空，後天晚上七點怎麼樣？ |
| 月 | 美 | ：好啊！再見。 |

## 課文拼音 Text in Pinyin

Āntóng　　: Yuèměi, nǐ yào qù nǎlǐ?

Yuèměi　　: Qù KTV chànggē. Wǒ hàn péngyǒu jiǔdiǎn èrshí fēn zài Dà'ān KTV
　　　　　　jiànmiàn.

Āntóng　　: Zǎoshàng jiǔdiǎn qù KTV? Wèishénme?

Yuèměi　　: Cóng zǎoshàng qīdiǎn dào zhōngwǔ shí'èrdiǎn, zuì piányí.
　　　　　　Yào bú yào yìqǐ qù?

Āntóng　　: Wǒ xiǎng qù, kěshì wǒ děi qù yínháng. Xià cì ba!

Yuèměi　　: Hǎo a, xià cì nǐ yídìng yào lái, wǒ xiǎng tīng nǐ chànggē.

Āntóng　　: Méi wèntí. Duìle, shénme shíhòu yǒu kòng yìqǐ chīfàn?

Yuèměi　　: Hòutiān wǒ yǒu kòng, nǐ ne?

Āntóng　　: Wǒ yě yǒu kòng, hòutiān wǎnshàng qīdiǎn zěnmeyàng?

Yuèměi　　: Hǎo a! Zàijiàn.

## 課文英譯 Text in English

Antong　　: Yuemei, where are you going?

Yuemei　　: To KTV to sing. My friends and I are meeting at Da-an KTV at 9:20.

Antong　　: Going to KTV at 9:00 in the morning? Why?

Yuemei　　: Because from 7:00 in the morning to 12 noon, it is the least expensive.
　　　　　　Do you want to go along?

Antong　　: I would love to, but I have to go to the bank. Maybe next time.

Yuemei　　: Okay. Next time, you have to come. I would like to hear you sing.

Antong　　: No problem. By the way, when do you have time to eat with me?

Yuemei　　: I'm free the day after tomorrow. Yourself?

Antong　　: I'm also free. How about the day after tomorrow at 7:00 in the evening?

Yuemei　　: Great. See you.

## 生詞一 Vocabulary 1  🎧 07-02

### Vocabulary

| 1 | 點 | diǎn | ㄉㄧㄢˇ | (M) | o'clock |
| 2 | KTV | | | (N) | Karaoke |
| 3 | 唱歌 | chànggē | ㄔㄤˋ ㄍㄜ | (V-sep) | to sing |
| 4 | 分 | fēn | ㄈㄣ | (M) | minute |
| 5 | 見面 | jiànmiàn | ㄐㄧㄢˋ ㄇㄧㄢˋ | (V-sep) | to meet |
| 6 | 從 | cóng | ㄘㄨㄥˊ | (Prep) | from |
| 7 | 中午 | zhōngwǔ | ㄓㄨㄥ ㄨˇ | (N) | noon |
| 8 | 得 | děi | ㄉㄟˇ | (Vaux) | to have to, must |
| 9 | 銀行 | yínháng | ㄧㄣˊ ㄏㄤˊ | (N) | bank |
| 10 | 時候 | shíhòu | ㄕˊ ㄏㄡˋ | (N) | when |
| 11 | 後天 | hòutiān | ㄏㄡˋ ㄊㄧㄢ | (N) | the day after tomorrow |

### Names

| 12 | 大安 | Dà'ān | ㄉㄚˋ ㄢ | | Da-an (name of a KTV named after a district in Taipei, where Shida is also located) |

### Phrases

| 13 | 下次 | xià cì | ㄒㄧㄚˋ ㄘˋ | | next time |
| 14 | 沒問題 | méi wèntí | ㄇㄟˊ ㄨㄣˋ ㄊㄧˊ | | No problem. |
| 15 | 對了 | duìle | ㄉㄨㄟˋ ㄌㄜ | | by the way |
| 16 | 有空 | yǒu kòng | ㄧㄡˇ ㄎㄨㄥˋ | | to have free time |
| 17 | 再見 | zàijiàn | ㄗㄞˋ ㄐㄧㄢˋ | | Goodbye. |

## 對話二 Dialogue **2**  07-03  07-B

安　同：如玉，妳在吃飯啊？

如　玉：是，吃午餐，等一下要上課。你呢？

安　同：我剛下課。對了，下午四點半學校有籃球
　　　　比賽。妳想去看嗎？

如　玉：想啊。比賽幾點結束？

安　同：六點半。妳晚上有事嗎？

如　玉：我最近很忙，每天晚上都上書法課。

安　同：學得怎麼樣？

如　玉：剛開始學，字寫得不好，可是我覺得很有意思。

安　同：我有空可以去看看嗎？

如　玉：我得問問老師。

## 課文拼音 Text in Pinyin

Āntóng　：Rúyù, nǐ zài chīfàn a?

Rúyù　：Shì, chī wǔcān, děng yíxià yào shàngkè. Nǐ ne?

Āntóng　：Wǒ gāng xiàkè. Duìle, xiàwǔ sìdiǎnbàn xuéxiào yǒu lánqiú bǐsài.
　　　　　Nǐ xiǎng qù kàn ma?

Rúyù　：Xiǎng a. Bǐsài jǐdiǎn jiéshù?

Āntóng　：Liùdiǎnbàn. Nǐ wǎnshàng yǒu shì ma?

Rúyù　：Wǒ zuìjìn hěn máng, měi tiān wǎnshàng dōu shàng shūfǎ kè.

Āntóng　：Xué de zěnmeyàng?

Rúyù　：Gāng kāishǐ xué, zì xiě de bù hǎo, kěshì wǒ juéde hěn yǒu yìsi.

Āntóng　：Wǒ yǒu kòng kěyǐ qù kànkàn ma?

Rúyù　：Wǒ děi wènwèn lǎoshī.

## 課文英譯 Text in English

Antong　：(I see) you're eating , Ruyu?

Ruyu　：Yeah, I'm eating lunch. I have class in a bit. How about you?

Antong　：I just got out of class. By the way, there is a basketball game at school at 4:30 this afternoon. Would you like to go watch?

Ruyu　：Yes, what time does the game end?

Antong　：6:30. Do you have something to do this evening?

Ruyu　：I have been busy lately. I go to calligraphy class every evening.

Antong　：How is that (the studying) going?

Ruyu　：I just started studying. I'm not writing characters well, but I think it is interesting.

Antong　：Can I go check it out sometime when I have free time?

Ruyu　：I have to ask the instructor.

## 生詞二 Vocabulary 2  07-04

## Vocabulary

| | | | | | |
|---|---|---|---|---|---|
| 1 | 在 | zài | ㄗㄞˋ | (Vs) | progressive aspect verb; in the process of doing something |
| 2 | 午餐 | wǔcān | ㄨˇ ㄘㄢ | (N) | lunch |
| 3 | 剛 | gāng | ㄍㄤ | (Adv) | just now |
| 4 | 下課 | xiàkè | ㄒㄧㄚˋ ㄎㄜˋ | (V-sep) | to finish class |
| 5 | 下午 | xiàwǔ | ㄒㄧㄚˋ ㄨˇ | (N) | afternoon |
| 6 | 半 | bàn | ㄅㄢˋ | (N) | half |
| 7 | 比賽 | bǐsài | ㄅㄧˇ ㄙㄞˋ | (N) | game, competition |
| 8 | 結束 | jiéshù | ㄐㄧㄝˊ ㄕㄨˋ | (Vp) | to finish |
| 9 | 最近 | zuìjìn | ㄗㄨㄟˋ ㄐㄧㄣˋ | (N) | recently, lately |
| 10 | 忙 | máng | ㄇㄤˊ | (Vs) | busy |
| 11 | 每 | měi | ㄇㄟˇ | (Det) | every, each |
| 12 | 天 | tiān | ㄊㄧㄢ | (M) | measure word for day |
| 13 | 書法 | shūfǎ | ㄕㄨ ㄈㄚˇ | (N) | calligraphy |
| 14 | 課 | kè | ㄎㄜˋ | (N) | class |
| 15 | 開始 | kāishǐ | ㄎㄞ ㄕˇ | (Vp) | to begin, to start |
| 16 | 字 | zì | ㄗˋ | (N) | character |
| 17 | 寫 | xiě | ㄒㄧㄝˇ | (V) | to write |
| 18 | 可以 | kěyǐ | ㄎㄜˇ ㄧˇ | (Vaux) | may (permission) |
| 19 | 問 | wèn | ㄨㄣˋ | (V) | to ask |

## Phrases

| | | | | | |
|---|---|---|---|---|---|
| 20 | 等一下 | děng yíxià | ㄉㄥˇ ㄧˊ ㄒㄧㄚˋ | | later |
| 21 | 有事 | yǒu shì | ㄧㄡˇ ㄕˋ | | to be busy, to be engaged |
| 22 | 有意思 | yǒu yìsi | ㄧㄡˇ ㄧˋ ㄙ | | to be interesting, to be fun |

## 文法 Grammar

### I. Time and Place of Events  07-05

拼音、英譯 p.44

**Function:** The time and place of events are often specified in sentences using the sequence Time + Place + Event. The subject of the sentence occurs either in front of or after Time.

1. 他和他朋友下午在教室寫書法。
2. 我昨天晚上到我家附近的咖啡店喝咖啡。
3. 我們這個週末去圖書館看書。
4. 你們明天早上十一點到我家來吃牛肉麵。

### Structures:

 **Negation:** The negative marker 不 *bù* appears before place elements.

1. 我晚上不在家吃飯。
2. 他和他哥哥最近都不來學校上課。
3. 他們這個週末不去山上看風景。

### Questions:

1. 你下午要不要來學校打籃球？
2. 你們現在在我家附近的商店買手機嗎？
3. 你朋友晚上幾點去 KTV 唱歌？
4. 他們什麼時候到花蓮看籃球比賽？
5. 你和你妹妹明天早上要去哪裡看電影？

### Usage:

1. Every event involves a time and a place. While the time and place may not be explicitly stated in the sentence, they are typically evident from the context. If there is no context, the references are 'right now' and 'right here'.

2. Note the word order. Time comes before place. For example, to express 'I don't eat dinner at home in the evening', we say 我晚上不在家吃飯。Wǒ wǎnshàng bú zài jiā chīfàn or 晚上我不在家吃飯。Wǎnshàng wǒ bú zài jiā chīfàn, but not *我不在家吃飯晚上 Wǒ bú zài jiā chīfàn wǎnshàng.

3. In Taiwan the sequence '去 ／ 來 + Place + VP' is interchangeable with '到 + Place + 去 ／ 來 + VP'. For example, 我們晚上去 KTV 唱歌。Wǒmen wǎnshàng qù KTV chànggē. 'We go to the KTV for singing in the evening' is the same as 我們晚上到 KTV 去唱歌。Wǒmen wǎnshàng dào KTV qù chànggē. The latter, however, is not as common as the former in Taiwan.

## 練習 Exercise

**Describe the pictures below by saying either Time or Place or both.**

| | |
|---|---|
|  | （晚上 ／ 他們家附近的餐廳 ／ 吃晚飯）<br>→ 他和他哥哥晚上七點在他們家附近的餐廳吃晚飯。 |
|  | （中午 ／ 圖書館 ／ 上網）<br>→ 他和他妹妹… |
|  | （下午 ／ 九樓的教室 ／ 寫書法）<br>→ 這三個學生… |
|  | （早上 ／ 學校 ／ 打籃球）<br>→ 很多學生… |

II. 從 cóng…到 dào… *from A to B*  07-06　　　　

**Function:** This pattern is used to indicate the "from...to..." spatial distance between two places and the "from...to..." temporal duration of an event. In other words, A and B can refer to times or places.

➊ 我從早上十點二十分到下午一點十分有中文課。
➋ 我今天從早上到晚上都有空，歡迎你們來我家。
➌ 從我家到那個游泳池有一點遠。
➍ 我從我朋友家到這個地方來。
➎ 他從圖書館到那家餐廳去吃飯。

**Structures:**

### ✎ Negation:

➊ 我們的書法課不是從九點到十一點。
➋ 陳先生的媽媽昨天不是從早上到晚上都很忙。
➌ A：我什麼時候可以去你家？
　　B：我今天從早上到晚上都沒有空。可是明天可以。
➍ 從這棟大樓到那家 KTV 不遠。
➎ 我不想從學校到那裡去，想從我家去。

### ✎ Questions: Three different patterns can be employed in this construction.

➊ 你們老師後天從早上到下午都有空嗎？（嗎）
➋ 請問從圖書館到你們宿舍遠不遠？（A-not-A）
➌ 他們想從宿舍還是圖書館到教室去上課？（A 還是 B）

## 練習 Exercise

Describe the events in the pictures.

**1**

姐姐 ＿＿＿＿＿＿＿ 在學校
看電影。

**2**

明天的游泳比賽 ＿＿＿＿＿
＿＿＿＿＿，歡迎你們來。

**3**

Q：從他家去那個商店遠不遠？
A：＿＿＿＿＿＿＿＿＿＿。

**4**

他從 ＿＿＿＿ 到 ＿＿＿＿ 去
＿＿＿＿＿。

## III. Progressive, On-going Actions 在 *zài* 🎧 07-07　🔍拼音、英譯 p.45

**Function:** 在 *zài* indicates an ongoing activity taking place at the present (default) or at a given time.

**1** 李老師在上課。　　**2** 你看！陳先生在唱歌。
**3** 昨天下午五點我在做飯。

## Structures:

✏️ **Negation:** Note that 不是 negation is more common than 不.

**1** 他不是在看書。他在看籃球比賽。
**2** 我不是在照相。我的手機不能照相。

 **Questions：**

① 你們在喝什麼？

② 他們老師在上課嗎？

③ 他們在打籃球嗎？

**Usage:** Only action verbs can be used with the 在 *zài* structure. State verbs cannot go with 在 *zài*. It is not correct to say *手機在貴 shǒujī zài guì.

---

**練習 Exercise**

**What are the people in his family doing?**

① 我在踢足球。

② 爸爸⋯

③ 媽媽⋯

④ 姐姐⋯

⑤ 弟弟⋯

---

**IV. 每 měi** *each and every* 🎧 07-08  拼音、英譯 p.46

**Function:** The Determiner 每 *měi* indicates each and every.

① 他妹妹每天都有空。

② 他朋友每個週末都去學校附近的游泳池游泳。

③ 每一棟大樓都可以上網。

④ 他家人，每個人都會做甜點。

**Structures:** Sentences with 每 *měi* almost always include the adverb 都 *dōu* 'all' to reinforce the sense of "no exception". 每 + M + N + 都 …. See the examples above.

✏ **Negation：**

1. The negation marker 不 *bù* or 沒 *méi* appears after 都 *dōu* but before the verb.

   (1) 他每天都不忙。

   (2) 我媽媽每個週末都沒空。

   (3) 這家商店，每支手機都不便宜。

2. To indicate 'it is not the case that...', 不是 *búshì* is used before 每（and also before 都 *dōu*）.

    **(1)** 他朋友不是每天都去看電影。

    **(2)** 我們不是每天都有書法課。

    **(3)** 他的兄弟姐妹不是每個人都喜歡打球。

## Questions:

  **1** 他每個週末都去哪裡運動？

  **2** 你爸爸每天都在家吃晚飯嗎？

  **3** 他的照片，每張都很好看嗎？

**Usage:** 每天 *měi tiān* is the same as 每一天 *měi yì tiān* 'every (single) day'. 一 *yī* 'one' is often omitted. Similarly, 每個 *měi ge* is the same as 每一個 *měi yí ge* 'every (single) one'.

---

## 練習 Exercise

Complete the sentences and dialogues below based on the pictures provided.

**1**

我哥哥每天…

**2**

每杯…

**3**

他的兄弟姐妹，每…

**4**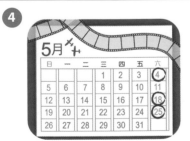

A：他每個週末都去看電影嗎？

B：＿＿＿＿＿＿＿＿＿＿＿。

**5**

A：他們學校，每棟大樓都很漂亮嗎？

B：＿＿＿＿＿＿＿＿＿＿＿。

## V. 可以 kěyǐ *permission*  07-09

拼音、英譯 p.47

**Function:** 可以 kěyǐ indicates permission to perform an action.

❶ 我媽媽說，你們可以來我家打籃球。
❷ 爸爸說，我可以買這支手機。
❸ 我叫馬安同，你可以叫我小馬。

**Structures:** 可以 kěyǐ is an auxiliary verb and it precedes the verb.

### ✎ Negation:

❶ 媽媽說，我不可以賣這支手機。
❷ 你不可以在圖書館裡面吃東西。
❸ 先生，對不起，你不可以在這裡照相。

### ✎ Questions:

❶ A：我可以不可以去看你們的籃球比賽？
　 B：沒問題！
❷ A：我想吃你的包子，可以嗎？
　 B：可以啊。
❸ A：這是你的書嗎？我可以看看嗎？
　 B：對不起，那不是我的書。

### Usage:

1. In Lesson 3 "看電影可以學中文。" Kàn diànyǐng kěyǐ xué Zhōngwén. "Watching movies, (I) can learn Chinese" and in Lesson 5 " 你可以教我嗎？ " Nǐ kěyǐ jiāo wǒ ma? "Can you teach me?", " 可以 " kěyǐ is used to inquire if it is possible for someone to do something. In this lesson, however, 可以 kěyǐ in the question 我有空可以去看看嗎？ Wǒ yǒu kòng kěyǐ qù kànkàn ma? "Can I go check it out when I have free time?" is used to ask for permission.

2. 不可以 can only be used to indicate "permission", not "possibility". The negative form can only be used to indicate permission. For example, " 你不可以說老闆不好。 " Nǐ bù kěyǐ shuō lǎobǎn bù hǎo. "You mustn't say anything bad about

the boss." When you use " 可不可以 " or " 可以不可以 ", it can indicate either permission or possibility. For example,

**(1)** 你可不可以明天來？(possibility)

**(2)** 我可以不可以買一支新手機？(permission)

3. When answering a question, " 可以 " alone suffices.

A：媽媽，我可不可以買這支手機？

B：可以。

---

### 練習 Exercise

Please complete the following dialogues using 可以 / 不可以 / 可不可以 / 可以嗎？.

**1** A：請問咖啡可以外帶嗎？

B：外帶、內用都 ＿＿＿＿＿＿＿＿＿＿＿。

**2** A：這杯烏龍茶是誰的？我 ＿＿＿＿＿＿＿＿＿＿ 喝嗎？

B：＿＿＿＿＿＿＿＿＿＿。請喝！

**3** A：請問我們可不可以在這裡打網球？

B：早上可以，可是晚上 ＿＿＿＿＿＿＿＿＿＿。

**4** A：這個週末我們 ＿＿＿＿＿＿＿＿＿＿ 去你家看看？

B：＿＿＿＿＿＿＿＿＿＿，我這個週末沒事。

**5** A：我們 ＿＿＿＿＿＿＿＿＿＿＿ 在大教室裡面吃東西嗎？

B：＿＿＿＿＿＿＿＿＿＿，可是小教室可以。

## 語法例句拼音與英譯
## Grammar Examples in Pinyin and English

## I.  Time and Place of Events

### Function:

1. Tā hàn tā péngyǒu xiàwǔ zài jiàoshì xiě shūfǎ.
2. Wǒ zuótiān wǎnshàng dào wǒ jiā fùjìn de kāfēi diàn hē kāfēi.
3. Wǒmen zhè ge zhōumò qù túshūguǎn kànshū.
4. Nǐmen míngtiān zǎoshàng shíyīdiǎn dào wǒ jiā lái chī niúròu miàn.

### Function:

1. He and his friends practice calligraphy in the afternoons in the classroom.
2. Last night, I went to a coffee shop near my house to have some coffee.
3. We will go to the library this weekend to study.
4. You guys come to my house to have beef noodles at 11:00 tomorrow morning.

### Structures:

🖉 Negation:

1. Wǒ wǎnshàng bú zài jiā chīfàn.

2. Tā hàn tā gēge zuìjìn dōu bù lái xuéxiào shàngkè.

3. Tāmen zhè ge zhōumò bú qù shānshàng kàn fēngjǐng.

### Structures:

🖉 Negation:

1. I don't eat dinner at home in the evenings.
2. He and his brother haven't come to school for classes lately.
3. They are not going up the mountain to view the scenery this weekend.

🖉 Questions:

1. Nǐ xiàwǔ yào bú yào lái xuéxiào dǎ lánqiú?
2. Nǐmen xiànzài zài wǒ jiā fùjìn de shāngdiàn mǎi shǒujī ma?
3. Nǐ péngyǒu wǎnshàng jǐdiǎn qù KTV chànggē?
4. Tāmen shénme shíhòu dào Huālián kàn lánqiú bǐsài?
5. Nǐ hàn nǐ mèimei míngtiān zǎoshàng yào qù nǎlǐ kàn diànyǐng?

🖉 Questions:

1. Would you like to come to school to play basketball in the afternoon?
2. Are you buying a cell phone in the shop near my house right now?
3. What time do your friends go to KTV to sing in the evening?
4. When are they going to Hualien to watch the basketball game?
5. Where are you and your sister going to go see the movie tomorrow morning?

## II.  從 cóng…到 dào… *from A to B*

### Function:

1. Wǒ cóng zǎoshàng shídiǎn èrshífēn dào xiàwǔ yìdiǎn shífēn yǒu Zhōngwén kè.

### Function:

1. I have Chinese class from 10:20am to 1:10pm.

**2** Wǒ jīntiān cóng zǎoshàng dào wǎnshàng dōu yǒu kòng, huānyíng nǐmen lái wǒ jiā.

**3** Cóng wǒ jiā dào nà ge yóuyǒngchí yǒu yìdiǎn yuǎn.

**4** Wǒ cóng wǒ péngyǒu jiā dào zhè ge dìfāng lái.

**5** Tā cóng túshūguǎn dào nà jiā cāntīng qù chīfàn.

**2** I am free from morning to night today. (You're) welcome to come to my house.

**3** From my house to that swimming pool is a little far.

**4** I came to this place from my friend's house.

**5** He went from the library to that restaurant to eat.

## Structures:

### ✏ Negation:

**1** Wǒmen de shūfǎ kè búshì cóng jiǔdiǎn dào shíyīdiǎn.

**2** Chén Xiānshēng de māma zuótiān búshì cóng zǎoshàng dào wǎnshàng dōu hěn máng.

**3** A: Wǒ shénme shíhòu kěyǐ qù nǐ jiā?
B: Wǒ jīntiān cóng zǎoshàng dào wǎnshàng dōu méi yǒu kòng, kěshì míngtiān kěyǐ.

**4** Cóng zhè dòng dàlóu dào nà jiā KTV bù yuǎn.

**5** Wǒ bù xiǎng cóng xuéxiào dào nàlǐ qù, xiǎng cóng wǒ jiā qù.

## Structures:

### ✏ Negation:

**1** Our calligraphy class is not from 9 to 11.

**2** Mr. Chen's mom wasn't busy yesterday from morning to night.

**3** A: When can I go to your house?
B: I don't have time from morning to night today, but tomorrow is OK.

**4** It is not far from this building to that KTV.

**5** I don't want to go there from school. I want to go from my house.

### ✏ Questions:

**1** Nǐmen lǎoshī hòutiān cóng zǎoshàng dào xiàwǔ dōu yǒu kòng ma?

**2** Qǐngwèn cóng túshūguǎn dào nǐmen sùshè yuǎn bù yuǎn?

**3** Tāmen xiǎng cóng sùshè háishì túshūguǎn dào jiàoshì qù shàngkè?

### ✏ Questions:

**1** Is your teacher free from morning to afternoon the day after tomorrow?

**2** Excuse me, is it far from the library to your dorm?

**3** Do they want to go from the dorm or from the library to the classroom for class?

## III. 在 zài  Progressive, On-going Actions

### Function:

**1** Lǐ Lǎoshī zài shàngkè.
**2** Nǐ kàn! Chén Xiānshēng zài chànggē.
**3** Zuótiān xiàwǔ wǔdiǎn wǒ zài zuòfàn.

### Function:

**1** Teacher Li is in class right now.
**2** Look! Mr. Chen is singing.
**3** I was cooking at 5:00 in the afternoon yesterday.

## Structures:

### 🖉 Negation:

1. Tā búshì zài kànshū. Tā zài kàn lánqiú bǐsài.
2. Wǒ búshì zài zhàoxiàng. Wǒ de shǒujī bù néng zhàoxiàng.

### 🖉 Questions:

1. Nǐmen zài hē shénme?
2. Tāmen lǎoshī zài shàngkè ma?
3. Tāmen zài dǎ lánqiú ma?

## Structures:

### 🖉 Negation:

1. He is not reading. He is watching a basketball game.
2. I am not taking a picture. My cellphone can't take photos.

### 🖉 Questions:

1. What are you drinking?
2. Is their teacher in class now?
3. Are they playing the basketball?

## IV. 每 měi *each and every*

### Function:

1. Tā mèimei měi tiān dōu yǒu kòng.
2. Tā péngyǒu měi ge zhōumò dōu qù xuéxiào fùjìn de yóuyǒngchí yóuyǒng.
3. Měi yí dòng dàlóu dōu kěyǐ shàngwǎng.
4. Tā jiārén, měi ge rén dōu huì zuò tiándiǎn.

### Function:

1. His sister is free every day.
2. His friend goes to the swimming pool near the school to swim every weekend.
3. The internet can be accessed from every building.
4. Everyone in his family can make desserts.

### Structures:

#### 🖉 Negation:

1. (1) Tā měi tiān dōu bù máng.
   (2) Wǒ māma měi ge zhōumò dōu méi kòng.
   (3) Zhè jiā shāngdiàn, měi zhī shǒujī dōu bù piányí.

2. (1) Tā péngyǒu búshì měi tiān dōu qù kàn diànyǐng.
   (2) Wǒmen búshì měi tiān dōu yǒu shūfǎ kè.
   (3) Tā de xiōngdì jiěmèi búshì měi ge rén dōu xǐhuān dǎ qiú.

### Structures:

#### 🖉 Negation:

1. (1) He gets lots of free time every day.
   (2) My mom is busy every weekend.

   (3) Every cellphone (sold) in this store is not cheap.

2. (1) His friend does not go to see a movie every day.
   (2) We don't have calligraphy class every day.
   (3) Not all his siblings like to play ball.

✏️ **Questions:**

1. Tā měi ge zhōumò dōu qù nǎlǐ yùndòng?
2. Nǐ bàba měi tiān dōu zài jiā chī wǎnfàn ma?
3. Tā de zhàopiàn, měi zhāng dōu hěn hǎokàn ma?

✏️ **Questions:**

1. Where does he go every weekend to exercise?
2. Does your dad eat dinner at home every day?
3. Does every one of his photos look nice?

## V. 可以 kěyǐ *permission*

### Function:

1. Wǒ māma shuō, nǐmen kěyǐ lái wǒ jiā dǎ lánqiú.
2. Bàba shuō, wǒ kěyǐ mǎi zhè zhī shǒujī.
3. Wǒ jiào Mǎ Āntóng, nǐ kěyǐ jiào wǒ Xiǎo Mǎ.

### Function:

1. My mom said you can come to my house to play basketball.
2. Dad said I can buy this cellphone.
3. My name is Ma An-tong. You can call me Xiao Ma.

### Structures:

✏️ **Negation:**

1. Māma shuō, wǒ bù kěyǐ mài zhè zhī shǒujī.
2. Nǐ bù kěyǐ zài túshūguǎn lǐmiàn chī dōngxi.
3. Xiānshēng, duìbùqǐ, nǐ bù kěyǐ zài zhèlǐ zhàoxiàng.

### Structures:

✏️ **Negation:**

1. Mom says I can't sell this cellphone.
2. You cannot eat in the library.
3. Sir, excuse me. You cannot take pictures here.

✏️ **Questions:**

1. A: Wǒ kěyǐ bù kěyǐ qù kàn nǐmen de lánqiú bǐsài?
   B: Méi wèntí!
2. A: Wǒ xiǎng chī nǐ de bāozi, kěyǐ ma?
   B: Kěyǐ a.
3. A: Zhè shì nǐ de shū ma? Wǒ kěyǐ kànkàn ma?
   B: Duìbùqǐ, nà búshì wǒ de shū.

✏️ **Questions:**

1. A: Can I go watch your basketball game?
   B: No problem.
2. A: I want to eat your baozi. Would that be okay?
   B: Sure.
3. A: Is this your book? Can I check it out?
   B: Sorry, that's not my book.

### Usage:

2. **(1)** Nǐ kě bù kěyǐ míngtiān lái?
   **(2)** Wǒ kěyǐ bù kěyǐ mǎi yì zhī xīn shǒujī?
3. A: Māma, wǒ kě bù kěyǐ mǎi zhè zhī shǒujī?
   B: Kěyǐ.

### Usage:

2. **(1)** Can you come tomorrow?
   **(2)** Can I buy a new cellphone?
3. A: Mom, can I buy this cellphone?
   B: Yes.

## 課室活動 Classroom Activities

### I. What Are They Doing?

**Goal:** Learning to describe an activity in progress.

**Task:** Please look at the pictures below and describe what they are doing and how well they are doing it.

### II. Daily Routines

**Goal:** Learning to describe actions that take place at certain points in time or during certain time frames.

**Task 1:** The table below shows 小明 Xiaoming's daily routine. Please refer to it to complete the sentences in the far right column.

| | | |
|---|---|---|
| 8:00am | | 他八點到學校來。 |
| 8:10~ 10:00am | | 他從 _____ 到 _____ 有中文課。 |
| 10:20~ 11:30am | | 他從 _____ 到 _____ 在教室 _____。 |
| 12:00~ 1:00pm | | 他和他朋友從 _____ 到 _____ 在學校附近的餐廳 _____。 |
| 3:30pm | | 他和他朋友… |

| 3:50~ 5:00pm |  | |
|---|---|---|

**Task 2:** Pair up with a classmate and take turns telling each other what each of you did yesterday. Report your findings to the class.

同學的名字：＿＿＿＿＿＿＿＿＿＿＿
Name of classmate

| 什麼時候<br>**When** | 在哪裡<br>**Where** | 做什麼<br>**What** |
|---|---|---|
| 早上 Morning | | |
| 中午 Noon | | |
| 下午 Afternoon | | |
| 晚上 Evening | | |

## III. Daily Activity Survey

**Goal:** Learning to talk about habitual actions. Learning to tell and ask about time.

**Task 1:** Interview your classmates and find out which of the following activities is something they do everyday. Write down their names and ask when they usually do these things.

| 每天做的事 | 名字 | 什麼時候做 |
|---|---|---|
| 喝咖啡 | | |
| 學中文 | | |
| 運動 | | |
| 上網 | | |
| 吃甜點 | | |
| 聽音樂 | | |
| 看電影 | | |

**Task 2:** What are some of the things that people in your family have to do every day or weekend?

## IV. Scheduling an Appointment

**Goal:** Learning to make an appointment with a friend.

**Task:** It is the weekend and you want to go out with your friend. Pair up with a classmate and write down your conversation. (Try to limit it to 10 sentences or less.) You may use the following words: 有空, 最近, 可以, 在哪裡, 什麼時候, 幾點.

## V. Advertisements

**Goal:** Learning to describe an activity in progress or that takes place, at a point in time or during a certain time frame.

**Task:** You see the following poster at school. Tell your classmates what you see and ask if they are interested. Other students can ask questions about the activity shown, such as training time and location.

# We Want You!!
## 龍舟隊
### (Dragon Boat Team)

❖ Requirements:
會游泳、會說一點中文

❖ 練習時間 Practice time:
每天 6:30~9:00 am

❖ 地方：新店 Xīndiàn

師大國語中心

# KTV — A Popular Leisure Activity in Taiwan

In Taiwan, singing is a very popular activity for people of all ages. Many people enjoy singing, at old-fashioned karaoke (KTV) bars and the more hip KTV chains. Some families even have a karaoke machine at home that allows them to sing whenever the mood strikes, or to invite friends over to join in on the fun. Some banquet venues even have a karaoke station where guests can sing whenever they like, thereby entertaining the other guests while they eat.

▲ KTV rooms

People don't need a reason to go sing. They do it in their free time for birthdays, or for other celebrations. Due to its popularity, newer KTV's are providing a wider range of services, including serving a wide selection of food and drinks to attract more customers.

▲ Food and drinks at karaoke bars

▲ Singing in KTVs　《聯合報》侯永全 / 攝影

# Notes on Pinyin and Pronunciation

**Pinyin Rules**

When the vowel "u" is followed by "en" and is preceded by a consonant, the "e" is omitted and the spelling becomes "-un". The "e", however, is still pronounced, e.g., jūn 君 in Lesson 2.

# Chinese Punctuation Marks

Chinese punctuation marks were designed based on the Western system. While a number of them are similar in forms and functions to their Western counterparts, some had been created locally, as shown below.

| | Marks | Pinyin | Functions |
|---|---|---|---|
| **Equivalents** | | | |
| 1 | ， | dòuhào | comma |
| 2 | ； | fēnhào | semicolon |
| 3 | ： | màohào | colon |
| 4 | ！ | jīngtànhào | exclamation |
| 5 | ？ | wènhào | question mark |
| 6 | （ ） | guāhào | parentheses |
| **Non-equivalents** | | | |
| 7 | 。 | jùhào | period |
| 8 | 「 」 | yǐnhào | single quotation mark |
| 9 | 『 』 | shuāngyǐnhào | double quotation mark |
| 10 | 、 | dùnhào | enumeration |
| 11 | …… | shānjiéhào | ellipsis |
| 12 | —— | pòzhéhào | em dash |
| 13 | ＿＿ | zhuānmínghào | name mark |
| 14 | ～～～ 《 》 | shūmínghào | title marks |
| 15 | 〈 〉 | piānmínghào | single title marks |
| 16 | · | jiàngéhào | separator mark |

## Self-Assessment Checklist

I can tell and ask about time.

20%        40%        60%        80%        100%

I can describe an activity that takes place at a point in time (time-when) or during a certain frame (time-duration).

20%        40%        60%        80%        100%

I can make appointments with friends.

20%        40%        60%        80%        100%

I can talk about a habitual activity.

20%        40%        60%        80%        100%

# LESSON

## 8

第八課

## 坐火車去臺南
### Taking a Train to Tainan

**學習目標 Learning Objectives**

**Topic:** 交通工具 Transportation

- Learning the names of different types of transportation and talking about getting to destinations.
- Learning to talk about some one's plans for their free time.
- Learning to make simple comparisons about various modes of transportation.
- Learning to explain likes and dislikes.

# LESSON 08

# 坐火車去臺南

# Taking a Train to Tainan

對話一 Dialogue 1 　　🎧 08-01  08-A

| 如 玉 ： | 這個週末，我想跟朋友去臺南玩。 |
| 明 華 ： | 怎麼去？ |
| 如 玉 ： | 我想坐火車去。 |
| 明 華 ： | 火車太慢了，要四個多鐘頭，坐高鐵比較快。 |
| 如 玉 ： | 可是聽說高鐵車票非常貴。 |
| 明 華 ： | 高鐵車票有一點貴，但是坐高鐵又快又舒服。 |
| 如 玉 ： | 我不知道在哪裡買票。 |
| 明 華 ： | 在高鐵站、網路上或是便利商店都可以。 |
| 如 玉 ： | 這麼方便！那我坐高鐵去，謝謝你。 |

## 課文拼音 Text in Pinyin

Rúyù : Zhè ge zhōumò, wǒ xiǎng gēn péngyǒu qù Táinán wán.

Mínghuá : Zěnme qù?

Rúyù : Wǒ xiǎng zuò huǒchē qù.

Mínghuá : Huǒchē tài màn le, yào sì ge duō zhōngtóu, zuò gāotiě bǐjiào kuài.

Rúyù : Kěshì tīngshuō gāotiě chēpiào fēicháng guì.

Mínghuá : Gāotiě chēpiào yǒu yìdiǎn guì, dànshì zuò gāotiě yòu kuài yòu shūfú.

Rúyù : Wǒ bù zhīdào zài nǎlǐ mǎi piào.

Mínghuá : Zài gāotiězhàn, wǎnglù shàng huòshì biànlì shāngdiàn dōu kěyǐ.

Rúyù : Zhème fāngbiàn! Nà wǒ zuò gāotiě qù, xièxie nǐ.

## 課文英譯 Text in English

Ruyu : I want to go to Tainan with friends this weekend.

Minghua : How are you going ?

Ruyu : I would like to go by train.

Minghua : The train is too slow. It takes more than 4 hours. Taking the High Speed Rail is faster.

Ruyu : But I've heard that the High Speed Rail tickets are very expensive.

Minghua : High Speed Rail tickets are a bit expensive, but the High Speed Rail is both fast and comfortable.

Ruyu : I don't know where to buy tickets.

Minghua : At High Speed Rail stations, online, or at convenience stores.

Ruyu : That is so convenient. Then I'll go by High Speed Rail. Thank you.

## 生詞一 Vocabulary 1  ⌒ 08-02

## Vocabulary

| 1 | 坐 | zuò | ㄗㄨㄛˋ | (V) | to take by, to travel by |
|---|---|---|---|---|---|
| 2 | 火車 | huǒchē | ㄏㄨㄛˇ ㄔㄜ | (N) | train |
| 3 | 跟 | gēn | ㄍㄣ | (Prep) | with |
| 4 | 玩 | wán | ㄨㄢˊ | (V) | to have fun |
| 5 | 怎麼 | zěnme | ㄗㄣˇ ㄇㄜ· | (Adv) | how |
| 6 | 慢 | màn | ㄇㄢˋ | (Vs) | slow |
| 7 | 鐘頭 | zhōngtóu | ㄓㄨㄥ ㄊㄡˊ | (N) | hour |
| 8 | 比較 | bǐjiào | ㄅㄧˇ ㄐㄧㄠˋ | (Adv) | (comparatively) more |
| 9 | 快 | kuài | ㄎㄨㄞˋ | (Vs) | fast |
| 10 | 車票 | chēpiào | ㄔㄜ ㄆㄧㄠˋ | (N) | (train, bus) ticket |
| 11 | 非常 | fēicháng | ㄈㄟ ㄔㄤˊ | (Adv) | very |
| 12 | 但是 | dànshì | ㄉㄢˋ ㄕˋ | (Conj) | but, however |
| 13 | 又 | yòu | ㄧㄡˋ | (Adv) | both...and... |
| 14 | 舒服 | shūfú | ㄕㄨ ㄈㄨˊ | (Vs) | comfortable |
| 15 | 站 | zhàn | ㄓㄢˋ | (N) | station |
| 16 | 或是 | huòshì | ㄏㄨㄛˋ ㄕˋ | (Conj) | or |

## Names

| 17 | 臺南 | Táinán | ㄊㄞˊ ㄋㄢˊ | | Tainan, a city in southwestern Taiwan |
| 18 | 高鐵 | gāotiě | ㄍㄠ ㄊㄧㄝˇ | | High Speed Rail (HSR) |

## Phrases

| 19 | 網路上 | wǎnglù shàng | ㄨㄤˇ ㄌㄨˋ ㄕㄤˋ | | on the Internet |
| 20 | 便利商店 | biànlì shāngdiàn | ㄅㄧㄢˋ ㄌㄧˋ ㄕㄤ ㄉㄧㄢˋ | | convenience store |

## 對話二 Dialogue 2  08-03  08-B

如　玉：安同，明天我們沒課，你想去哪裡？

安　同：我要跟同學去參觀故宮博物院。

如　玉：聽說那裡有很多中國古代的東西。

安　同：是啊。妳要跟我們去看看嗎？

如　玉：好。怎麼去？

安　同：我同學騎機車載我。妳可以坐公共汽車去。

如　玉：我想坐捷運去。比較快。

安　同：不行，到故宮沒有捷運。妳要不要坐計程車去？

如　玉：太貴了！我坐公車。騎機車比坐公車快嗎？

安　同：差不多。

## 課文拼音 Text in Pinyin

Rúyù : Āntóng, míngtiān wǒmen méi kè, nǐ xiǎng qù nǎlǐ?

Āntóng : Wǒ yào gēn tóngxué qù cānguān Gùgōng Bówùyuàn.

Rúyù : Tīngshuō nàlǐ yǒu hěn duō Zhōngguó gǔdài de dōngxi.

Āntóng : Shì a. Nǐ yào gēn wǒmen qù kànkàn ma?

Rúyù : Hǎo. Zěnme qù?

Āntóng : Wǒ tóngxué qí jīchē zài wǒ. Nǐ kěyǐ zuò gōnggòng qìchē qù.

Rúyù : Wǒ xiǎng zuò jiéyùn qù. Bǐjiào kuài.

Āntóng : Bù xíng, dào Gùgōng méi yǒu jiéyùn. Nǐ yào bú yào zuò jìchéngchē qù?

Rúyù : Tài guì le! Wǒ zuò gōngchē. Qí jīchē bǐ zuò gōngchē kuài ma?

Āntóng : Chābùduō.

## 課文英譯 Text in English

Ruyu : Antong, we don't have class tomorrow. Where do you want to go?

Antong : I am going to go to the Palace Museum with my classmates.

Ruyu : I've heard that there are a lot of ancient Chinese things there.

Antong : Yes. Would you like to go with us to check it out?

Ruyu : OK. How are you going?

Antong : My classmate is taking me on his scooter. You can take the bus.

Ruyu : I want to take the MRT. It is faster.

Antong : Won't work. There is no MRT to the Palace Museum. Do you want to take a taxi?

Ruyu : Too expensive. I'll take the bus. Is it faster to ride a scooter than to take the bus?

Antong : About the same.

# 生词二 Vocabulary 　 08-04

## Vocabulary

| | | | | | |
|---|---|---|---|---|---|
| 1 | 同學 | tóngxué | ㄊㄨㄥˊ ㄒㄩㄝˊ | (N) | classmate |
| 2 | 參觀 | cānguān | ㄘㄢ ㄍㄨㄢ | (V) | to visit (an institution) |
| 3 | 古代 | gǔdài | ㄍㄨˇ ㄉㄞˋ | (N) | ancient times |

| 4 | 騎 | qí | ㄑㄧˊ | (V) | to ride |
| 5 | 機車 | jīchē | ㄐㄧ ㄔㄜ | (N) | motorcycle, scooter |
| 6 | 載 | zài | ㄗㄞˋ | (V) | to give someone a ride (on / in a vehicle, e.g. motorcycle, bicycle or car) |
| 7 | 捷運 | jiéyùn | ㄐㄧㄝˊ ㄩㄣˋ | (N) | Mass Rapid Transit (MRT) |
| 8 | 比 | bǐ | ㄅㄧˇ | (Prep) | (more...) than |

## Names

| 9 | 故宮博物院（故宮） | Gùgōng Bówùyuàn | ㄍㄨˋ ㄍㄨㄥ ㄅㄛˊ ㄨˋ ㄩㄢˋ | | National Palace Museum |
| 10 | 中國 | Zhōngguó | ㄓㄨㄥ ㄍㄨㄛˊ | | China |

## Phrases

| 11 | 公共汽車（公車） | gōnggòng qìchē | ㄍㄨㄥ ㄍㄨㄥˋ ㄑㄧˋ ㄔㄜ | | bus |
| 12 | 不行 | bù xíng | ㄅㄨˋ ㄒㄧㄥˊ | | will not do |
| 13 | 計程車 | jìchéngchē | ㄐㄧˋ ㄔㄥˊ ㄔㄜ | | taxi |
| 14 | 差不多 | chābùduō | ㄔㄚ ㄅㄨˋ ㄉㄨㄛ | | about the same |

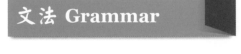

文法 Grammar

## I. Companionship with 跟 gēn 🎧 08-05

拼音、英譯 p.70

**Function:** The preposition 跟 *gēn* introduces somebody one does something with.

❶ 我常跟哥哥去看棒球比賽。

❷ 我跟朋友在餐廳吃飯。

❸ 我週末要跟同學去參觀故宮。

**Structures:** The ' 跟 *gēn* + somebody' expression appears before the VP as do all prepositional phrases. The adverb 一起 *yìqǐ* is commonly associated with 跟 *gēn* and is placed in front of the main verb.

**Negation:** The negation marker 不 *bù* appears before 跟 *gēn*.

1. 我今天不跟同學去上書法課。
2. 他不跟我一起去 KTV 唱歌。
3. 妹妹不跟我去吃越南菜。

**Questions:**

1. 你要跟他去日本嗎？
2. 你常跟誰去看電影？
3. 你想跟我去打網球嗎？
4. 你跟不跟我去圖書館看書？

## 練習 Exercise

Take turns asking and answering the following questions.

| | A（問） | B（答） |
|---|---|---|
| 1 | 你喜歡跟誰去玩？ | 我喜歡跟＿＿＿＿＿＿＿＿。 |
| 2 | 你想跟誰去看電影？ | 我想跟＿＿＿＿＿＿＿＿。 |
| 3 | 你要跟誰去打籃球？ | 我要跟＿＿＿＿＿＿＿＿。 |
| 4 | 你常跟誰吃晚飯？ | 我常跟＿＿＿＿＿＿＿＿。 |
| 5 | 你跟他在做什麼？ | 我跟他在＿＿＿＿＿＿。 |
| 6 | 你跟你哥哥去看棒球比賽嗎？ | 我不跟＿＿＿＿＿＿去，<br>我跟＿＿＿＿＿去。 |
| 7 | 你跟他去吃牛肉麵嗎？ | 我＿＿＿＿＿＿，我在家吃飯。 |

## II. Asking How with 怎麼 zěnme  08-06

 拼音、英譯 p.70

**Function:** 怎麼 *zěnme*, 'how?', is a question adverb, used to ask how something is done.

**❶** 你們怎麼去？

**❷** 這個菜怎麼做？

**❸** 這個歌怎麼唱？

**❹** 這支新手機怎麼上網？

**Usage:** 怎麼 'How?' is quite different from 怎麼樣 'How is it? / What do you think?' 怎麼 is an adverb, whereas 怎麼樣 is a state verb. Compare 這個菜怎麼做？ Zhè ge cài zěnme zuò? 'How is this dish made?' with 這個菜怎麼樣？ Zhè ge cài zěnmeyàng? 'How is this dish? / What do you think of this dish?'

### 練習 Exercise

Describe the manner of action to be carried out in the situations given below.

安同可以怎麼去 學校 / 臺南 / 故宮 / 朋友家？

### III. Implicit Comparison with 比較 bǐjiào  08-07  拼音、英譯 p.71

**Function:** The adverb 比較 *bǐjiào* conveys implicit comparison. The comparison is understood based on the context.

**①** 今天比較熱。

**②** 越南餐廳很遠。坐捷運比較快。

**③** 我們家，姐姐比較會做飯。

**Structures:** Adverbs do not take negation directly. Negation goes with the main verb.

🖉 **Negation:**

**①** 昨天比較不熱。

**②** 他比較不喜歡游泳。

**③** 我最近比較沒有空。

🖉 **Questions:**

**①** 咖啡和茶，你比較喜歡喝咖啡嗎？

**②** 你和哥哥，你比較會打棒球嗎？

**③** 他比較想去看美國電影還是日本電影？

**Usage:** In mainland China, 比較 *bǐjiào* can be used as an adverb meaning 'quite, rather' without a sense of comparison. 他的法文說得比較好。 Tā de Fǎwén shuō de bǐjiào hǎo. 'He speaks French rather well.' In Taiwan, 比較 *bǐjiào* always indicates a comparison. 哥哥和我，我比較高。 Gēge hàn wǒ, wǒ bǐjiào gāo. 'Between me and my brother, I am taller.'

### 練習 Exercise

Make sentences with 比較 *bǐjiào* by using the words given in the parentheses. E.g., 坐計程車比較快。 Zuò jìchéngchē bǐjiào kuài. (It would be faster to take a taxi (to get there).)

| ① | ② | ③ |
|---|---|---|
|  |  |  |
| 快 | 常 | 喜歡 |

  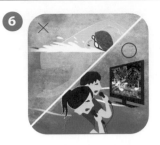

| 舒服 | 慢 | 有意思 |

**IV.** 又 yòu⋯ 又 yòu⋯ *both A and B*  🎧 08-08

🔍 拼音、英譯 p.71

**Function:** The pattern　又 yòu⋯ 又 yòu⋯ "both A and B" is used to indicate two qualities, situations, or behaviors that are true of the person or thing being discussed.

❶ 這家餐廳的菜，又便宜又好吃，所以我們常來吃。
❷ 坐高鐵又快又舒服，可是有一點貴。
❸ 我又想喝茶又想喝咖啡，但是這裡沒有便利商店。

**Structures:** 又＋Vs＋又＋Vs.

✏️ **Negation:** The negation marker　不 bù appears after both the first　又 yòu

and the second 又 yòu, forming 又不 yòu bù⋯又不 yòu bù⋯.

❶ 老闆今天做的臭豆腐，又不臭又不辣。我覺得不好吃。
❷ 我的舊手機又不能照相又不能上網。我想買新的。

**練習 Exercise**

Complete the dialogues below using the 又⋯又⋯ pattern.

❶ A：這家咖啡店的咖啡怎麼樣？
　　B：＿＿＿＿＿＿＿＿＿＿＿＿＿＿＿。（便宜、好喝）

❷ A：你覺得這個電影怎麼樣？
　　B：＿＿＿＿＿＿＿＿＿＿＿＿＿＿＿。（好看、有意思）

**③** A：我們週末去運動還是在家看書？

B：＿＿＿＿＿＿＿＿＿＿＿＿，我們去 KTV 唱歌。
（不想…不想…）

**④** A：你為什麼不買這種手機？

B：＿＿＿＿＿＿＿＿＿＿＿＿。（不好看、不能上網）

**⑤** A：這種甜點好吃嗎？

B：＿＿＿＿＿＿＿＿＿＿＿＿。（好吃、便宜）

## V. Comparison with 比 bǐ 🎧 08-09

拼音、英譯 p.72

**Function:** The 比 *bǐ* preposition indicates an explicit comparison between two items.

**❶** 山上的風景比這裡漂亮。 **❷** 我們學校比他們學校遠。
**❸** 坐捷運比坐火車快。

**Structures:** A 比 B Vs.

**Negation:** The 比 pattern can be negated by either 不 *bù* or 不是 *búshì*.

**❶** 在家上網不比在學校快。
**❷** 我的車不比他的車貴。
**❸** 坐公車不是比坐計程車快。

**Questions:**

**❶** 他們學校比你們學校遠嗎？
**❷** 這種手機比那種貴嗎？

**Usage:** In the 比 *bǐ* pattern, degree adverbs like 很 *hěn* 'very', 真 *zhēn* 'really', and 非常 *fēicháng* 'extraordinary' do not appear before the Vs. It is incorrect, therefore, to say:

*我的手機比他的很貴。　　*坐高鐵比坐火車非常快。

### 練習 Exercise

Use the vocabulary you learned to compare the situations given in the pictures.

Example

A：週末你想去看電影還是去 KTV 唱歌？
為什麼？

B：我想去 KTV 唱歌。我覺得去 KTV 唱歌比看電影有意思。

有意思、好玩、快、慢、便宜、貴、美…

1

2

3

100元

70元

4

語法例句拼音與英譯
## Grammar Examples in Pinyin and English

## I. Companionship with 跟 gēn

### Function:

1. Wǒ cháng gēn gēge qù kàn bàngqiú bǐsài.
2. Wǒ gēn péngyǒu zài cāntīng chīfàn.
3. Wǒ zhōumò yào gēn tóngxué qù cānguān Gùgōng.

### Function:

1. I often go see baseball games with my brother.
2. I am having a meal at a restaurant with friends.
3. I'm going to go visit the Palace Museum this weekend with a classmate.

### Structures:

🖊 **Negation:**

1. Wǒ jīntiān bù gēn tóngxué qù shàng shūfǎ kè.
2. Tā bù gēn wǒ yìqǐ qù KTV chànggē.
3. Mèimei bù gēn wǒ qù chī Yuènán cài.

🖊 **Questions:**

1. Nǐ yào gēn tā qù Rìběn ma?
2. Nǐ cháng gēn shéi qù kàn diànyǐng?
3. Nǐ xiǎng gēn wǒ qù dǎ wǎngqiú ma?
4. Nǐ gēn bù gēn wǒ qù túshūguǎn kànshū?

### Structures:

🖊 **Negation:**

1. I am not going to go to the calligraphy class with my classmate today.
2. He isn't going to go to KTV with me.
3. My sister isn't going to go with me to have Vietnamese food.

🖊 **Questions:**

1. Are you going to go to Japan with him?
2. Who do you often go with to see movies?
3. Do you want to go with me to play tennis?
4. Are you going to go with me to the library to study?

## II. Asking How with 怎麼 zěnme

### Function:

1. Nǐmen zěnme qù?
2. Zhè ge cài zěnme zuò?
3. Zhè ge gē zěnme chàng?
4. Zhè zhī xīn shǒujī zěnme shàngwǎng?

### Function:

1. How do you go there?
2. How do you make this dish?
3. How do you sing this song?
4. How do I access the internet using this new cellphone?

## III. Implicit Comparison with 比較 bǐjiào

### Function:

① Jīntiān bǐjiào rè.

② Yuènán cāntīng hěn yuǎn. Zuò jiéyùn bǐjiào kuài.

③ Wǒmen jiā, jiějie bǐjiào huì zuòfàn.

### Function:

① Today is relatively hot.

② The Vietnamese restaurant is very far. Taking the MRT would be faster.

③ In our family, my elder sister cooks better.

### Structures:

🖊 **Negation:**

① Zuótiān bǐjiào bú rè.

② Tā bǐjiào bù xǐhuān yóuyǒng.

③ Wǒ zuìjìn bǐjiào méi yǒu kòng.

🖊 **Negation:**

① Yesterday was less hot.

② He doesn't like swimming as much (compared to some other activity or to someone else.)

③ I have been relatively busy lately.

🖊 **Questions:**

① Kāfēi hàn chá, nǐ bǐjiào xǐhuān hē kāfēi ma?

② Nǐ hàn gēge, nǐ bǐjiào huì dǎ bàngqiú ma?

③ Tā bǐjiào xiǎng qù kàn Měiguó diànyǐng háishì Rìběn diànyǐng?

🖊 **Questions:**

① Coffee and tea, do you prefer drinking coffee?

② Between you and your older brother, do you play baseball better?

③ Would he prefer to go watch an American movie or a Japanese movie?

## IV. 又 yòu… 又 yòu… *both A and B*

### Function:

① Zhè jiā cāntīng de cài, yòu piányí yòu hǎochī, suǒyǐ wǒmen cháng lái chī.

② Zuò gāotiě yòu kuài yòu shūfú, kěshì yǒu yìdiǎn guì.

③ Wǒ yòu xiǎng hē chá yòu xiǎng hē kāfēi, dànshì zhèlǐ méi yǒu biànlì shāngdiàn.

### Function:

① The food in this restaurant is both inexpensive and delicious, so we often eat here.

② Taking the High Speed Rail is both fast and comfortable, but it's a little expensive.

③ I want to drink both tea and coffee, but there are no convenience stores here.

### Structures:

🖊 **Negation:**

① Lǎobǎn jīntiān zuò de chòu dòufǔ yòu bú chòu yòu bú là. Wǒ juéde bù hǎochī.

② Wǒ de jiù shǒujī yòu bù néng zhàoxiàng yòu bù néng shàngwǎng. Wǒ xiǎng mǎi xīn de.

### Structures:

🖊 **Negation:**

① The stinky tofu that the vendor made today tastes neither stinky nor spicy. I don't think it tastes any good.

② My old cellphone cannot take photos, nor can it go online. I want to buy a new one.

# V. Comparison with 比 bǐ

## Function：

**1** Shānshàng de fēngjǐng bǐ zhèlǐ piàoliàng.

**2** Wǒmen xuéxiào bǐ tāmen xuéxiào yuǎn.

**3** Zuò jiéyùn bǐ zuò huǒchē kuài.

## Function：

**1** The view on the mountain is more beautiful than here.

**2** Our school is farther away than their school.

**3** Taking the MRT is faster than taking the train.

## Structures:

### Negation:

**1** Zài jiā shàngwǎng bù bǐ zài xuéxiào kuài.

**2** Wǒ de chē bù bǐ tā de chē guì.

**3** Zuò gōngchē búshì bǐ zuò jìchéngchē kuài.

### Negation:

**1** Using the internet at home is not faster than using it at school.

**2** My car is not more expensive than his.

**3** Taking the bus is not faster than taking a taxi.

### Questions:

**1** Tāmen xuéxiào bǐ nǐmen xuéxiào yuǎn ma?

**2** Zhè zhǒng shǒujī bǐ nà zhǒng guì ma?

### Questions:

**1** Is their school farther away than your school?

**2** Is this kind of cellphone more expensive than that kind?

課 室 活 動 **Classroom Activities**

## I. Making Arrangements

**Goal:** Learning to talk about your plans in your free time.
**Task:** Pretend to make plans with your family or friends, fill in the following time slots with your plans, then talk about your plans.

Example

今天下午我要跟媽媽坐公車到學校附近去吃越南菜。

| 什麼時候 | 跟誰 | 怎麼去 | 去哪裡 | 做什麼事 |
|---|---|---|---|---|
| 今天下午 | 媽媽 | 坐公車 | 學校附近 | 吃越南菜 |
| 今天晚上 | | | | |
| 明天中午 | | | | |
| 明天晚上 | | | | |
| 這個週末 | | | | |

## II. Tell Us What You Think

**Goal:** Learning to explain what somebody likes or dislikes about something.

**Task:** Your classmate likes to ask you "why?". Please give him/her at least two reasons, e.g.,

A：為什麼你喜歡喝烏龍茶？

B：烏龍茶又好喝又便宜，所以我喜歡。

**❶** 你為什麼常坐高鐵？

**❷** 你為什麼要買這種手機？

**❸** 你為什麼不吃那家的牛肉麵？

250元

**❹** 你為什麼喜歡這個電影？

好看、有意思

## III. Which Is Better?

**Goal:** Learning to make simple comparisons.

**Task:** The following are a few activities that you and your classmates could do over the weekend. Have a discussion, decide what to do, and tell the class what your final plans are and why you picked the activity you picked. Please use '比' or '比較' to tell the reasons.

## IV. How Do You Plan on Getting There?

**Goal:** Learning to say the different types of transportation and talk about getting to destinations.

**Task:** Your friend/family is coming to Taiwan to visit you. You want to take them to 陽明山. Please tell us how you plan on getting there.

## 文化 *Bits of Chinese Culture*

### Souvenirs

When people travel or return to their hometowns, they buy local products as gifts for friends and family. This is part of Chinese culture and tradition. To help promote tourism, local governments in Taiwan encourage the sale of items that exhibit special local characteristics, such as unique foods and clothing and which can help boost the local economy. Popular souvenirs include various sweets and snacks, agricultural, seafood, mining, and farm products, items of historical significance, such as tea from 阿里山 *Ālǐshān* (Ali Mountain,) pineapple cakes, sun cakes, Hualien marble, Taiwan corals, and T-shirts and key chains emblazoned with images of Taiwan.

▲ Pinapple cakes

▲ Key chains

▲ Snacks

▲ T-shirts

▲ Magnets

▲ Tea bags

照片授權攝影：台北 101

# YouBike in Taipei

YouBike is Taipei's public bicycle rental system. The unmanned system is managed digitally and is available 24 hours a day. YouBike leverages the facts that bikes are eco-friendly, cost-effective, and a convenient way to connect between different modes of transport to encourage the public to drive less and use public transportation more.

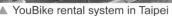

▲ YouBike rental system in Taipei

▲ Kiosk for renting bicycles

# Notes on Pinyin and Pronunciation

### Pinyin Rules

When the vowel "i" is followed by "ang" but is not preceded by a consonant, the "i" is changed to "y." When "i" is followed by "eng" and is not preceded by a consonant, the "e" is omitted to become "ying".

## Self-Assessment Checklist

I can say different types of transportation and talk about getting to destinations.

20%　　40%　　60%　　80%　　100%

I can talk about a person's plans in his free time.

20%　　40%　　60%　　80%　　100%

I can make a simple comparisons of various types of transportation.

20%　　40%　　60%　　80%　　100%

I can explain what somebody likes or dislikes about something.

20%　　40%　　60%　　80%　　100%

# LESSON
## 9

### 第九課

# 放假去哪裡玩？
## Where Will You Go for the Holidays?

**學習目標 Learning Objectives**

**Topic: 休閒 Leisure**

- Learning to use time expressions to describe events.
- Learning to discuss travel plans with friends.
- Learning to talk about hypothetical situations.
- Learning to give suggestions about leisure activities.

# 放假去哪裡玩？

## Where Will You Go for the Holidays?

| | | |
|---|---|---|
| 安 | 同 | ：田中，下個星期我們放五天的假，你要回國嗎？ |
| 田 | 中 | ：不，我打算在家看電視、影片學中文，你呢？ |
| 安 | 同 | ：我想跟朋友去玩。 |
| 田 | 中 | ：不錯啊。去什麼地方？ |
| 安 | 同 | ：臺東。聽說那裡的風景非常漂亮。 |
| 田 | 中 | ：我也聽說。放假的時候，你常去旅行嗎？ |
| 安 | 同 | ：不一定。有時候在家寫功課，有時候出去玩。 |
| 田 | 中 | ：你們什麼時候去臺東？ |
| 安 | 同 | ：這個星期六下午去。 |
| 田 | 中 | ：去玩多久？ |
| 安 | 同 | ：大概玩四、五天。 |

## 課文拼音 Text in Pinyin

Āntóng : Tiánzhōng, xià ge xīngqí wǒmen fàng wǔ tiān de jià, nǐ yào huíguó ma?

Tiánzhōng: Bù, wǒ dǎsuàn zài jiā kàn diànshì, yǐngpiàn xué Zhōngwén, nǐ ne?

Āntóng : Wǒ xiǎng gēn péngyǒu qù wán.

Tiánzhōng: Búcuò a. Qù shénme dìfāng?

Āntóng : Táidōng. Tīngshuō nàlǐ de fēngjǐng fēicháng piàoliàng.

Tiánzhōng: Wǒ yě tīngshuō. Fàngjià de shíhòu, nǐ cháng qù lǚxíng ma?

Āntóng : Bù yídìng. Yǒu shíhòu zài jiā xiě gōngkè, yǒu shíhòu chūqù wán.

Tiánzhōng: Nǐmen shénme shíhòu qù Táidōng?

Āntóng : Zhè ge xīngqíliù xiàwǔ qù.

Tiánzhōng: Qù wán duō jiǔ?

Āntóng : Dàgài wán sì, wǔ tiān.

## 課文英譯 Text in English

Antong : Tianzhong, we are having a five-day break next week. Are you going back to your country?

Tianzhong: No. I plan on staying home and watching television and films to study Chinese. And you?

Antong : I want to go out with my friends.

Tianzhong: That sounds good. Go where?

Antong : Taitung. I've heard the scenery there is very pretty.

Tianzhong: I've heard that, too. Do you often travel on days off?

Antong : Not necessarily. Sometimes, I stay home to do homework. Sometimes, I go out.

Tianzhong: When will you go to Taitung?

Antong : (We're) going this Saturday afternoon.

Tianzhong: How long will you be there?

Antong : Probably four or five days.

## 生詞一 Vocabulary 1  09-02

### Vocabulary

| 1 | 星期 + number | xīngqí | ㄒㄧㄥ ㄑㄧˊ | (N) | week |
| 2 | 回國 | huíguó | ㄏㄨㄟˊ ㄍㄨㄛˊ | (V-sep) | to return to one's country |
| 3 | 打算 | dǎsuàn | ㄉㄚˇ ㄙㄨㄢˋ | (Vaux) | to plan to |
| 4 | 電視 | diànshì | ㄉㄧㄢˋ ㄕˋ | (N) | TV |
| 5 | 影片 | yǐngpiàn | ㄧㄥˇ ㄆㄧㄢˋ | (N) | film |
| 6 | 旅行 | lǚxíng | ㄌㄩˇ ㄒㄧㄥˊ | (Vi) | to travel |
| 7 | 功課 | gōngkè | ㄍㄨㄥ ㄎㄜˋ | (N) | homework |
| 8 | 出去 | chūqù | ㄔㄨ ㄑㄩˋ | (Vi) | to go out |
| 9 | 大概 | dàgài | ㄉㄚˋ ㄍㄞˋ | (Adv) | approximately, about, probably |

### Phrases

| 10 | 放假 | fàngjià | ㄈㄤˋ ㄐㄧㄚˋ | | to have a holiday |
| 11 | 下個星期 | xià ge xīngqí | ㄒㄧㄚˋ ㄍㄜ ㄒㄧㄥ ㄑㄧˊ | | next week |
| 12 | 有時候 | yǒu shíhòu | ㄧㄡˇ ㄕˊ ㄏㄡˋ | | sometimes |
| 13 | 多久 | duō jiǔ | ㄉㄨㄛ ㄐㄧㄡˇ | | how long |

### Names

| 14 | 臺東 | Táidōng | ㄊㄞˊ ㄉㄨㄥ | | Taitung, name of one of the major cities on the southeastern coast of Taiwan |

對話二 Dialogue 2  09-03  09-B

| | | |
|---|---|---|
| 田 | 中 | ：我女朋友九月三十號要來臺灣看我。 |
| 明 | 華 | ：你想帶她去哪裡玩？ |
| 田 | 中 | ：還不知道。你有什麼建議？ |
| 明 | 華 | ：臺灣的夜市很有名。你們應該去逛逛。 |
| 田 | 中 | ：謝謝，還有什麼好玩的地方？ |
| 明 | 華 | ：臺灣的茶也很特別。臺北有很多茶館。 |
| 田 | 中 | ：到哪裡喝茶比較好？ |
| 明 | 華 | ：你們可以去貓空。那裡的風景很美。 |
| 田 | 中 | ：謝謝你。我決定帶她去貓空。<br>你也一起去，好不好？ |
| 明 | 華 | ：要是那時候我有空，就跟你們一起去。 |
| 田 | 中 | ：太好了！謝謝！ |

## 課文拼音 Text in Pinyin

Tiánzhōng: Wǒ nǚ péngyǒu jiǔyuè sānshíhào yào lái Táiwān kàn wǒ.

Mínghuá　: Nǐ xiǎng dài tā qù nǎlǐ wán?

Tiánzhōng: Hái bù zhīdào. Nǐ yǒu shénme jiànyì?

Mínghuá　: Táiwān de yèshì hěn yǒumíng. Nǐmen yīnggāi qù guàngguàng.

Tiánzhōng: Xièxie, hái yǒu shénme hǎowán de dìfāng?

Mínghuá　: Táiwān de chá yě hěn tèbié. Táiběi yǒu hěn duō cháguǎn.

Tiánzhōng: Dào nǎlǐ hē chá bǐjiào hǎo?

Mínghuá　: Nǐmen kěyǐ qù Māokōng. Nàlǐ de fēngjǐng hěn měi.

Tiánzhōng: Xièxie nǐ. Wǒ juédìng dài tā qù Māokōng. Nǐ yě yìqǐ qù, hǎo bù hǎo?

Mínghuá　: Yàoshì nà shíhòu wǒ yǒu kòng, jiù gēn nǐmen yìqǐ qù.

Tiánzhōng: Tài hǎo le! Xièxie!

## 課文英譯 Text in English

Tianzhong: My girlfriend is coming to Taiwan on September 30th to see me.

Minghua　: Where do you plan to take her?

Tianzhong: Don't know yet. Do you have any suggestions?

Minghua　: Taiwan's night markets are famous. You should go to the night market.

Tianzhong: Thank you. What other places are fun?

Minghua　: Taiwanese tea is also very special. Taipei has many tea houses.

Tianzhong: Where's a good place to go have tea?

Minghua　: You could go to Maokong. The scenery there is beautiful.

Tianzhong: Thank you. I've decided to take her to Maokong. You come with us, okay?

Minghua　: If I am free at that time, then I will go with you.

Tianzhong: Great! Thank you!

## 生词二 Vocabulary 2  09-04

## Vocabulary

| 1 | 女 + noun | nǚ | ㄋㄩˇ | (N) | girl-, female- |
|---|---|---|---|---|---|
| 2 | number + 月 | yuè | ㄩㄝˋ | (N) | month of a year |
| 3 | number + 號 | hào | ㄏㄠˋ | (N) | date, day of a month |
| 4 | 帶 | dài | ㄉㄞˋ | (V) | to take |
| 5 | 她 | tā | ㄊㄚ | (N) | she, her |
| 6 | 還 | hái | ㄏㄞˊ | (Adv) | still, additionally |
| 7 | 建議 | jiànyì | ㄐㄧㄢˋ ㄧˋ | (N) | suggestion |
| 8 | 夜市 | yèshì | ㄧㄝˋ ㄕˋ | (N) | night market |
| 9 | 應該 | yīnggāi | ㄧㄥ ㄍㄞ | (Vaux) | should |
| 10 | 逛 | guàng | ㄍㄨㄤˋ | (V) | to wander around, to look around |
| 11 | 特別 | tèbié | ㄊㄜˋ ㄅㄧㄝˊ | (Vs) | special |
| 12 | 茶館 | cháguǎn | ㄔㄚˊ ㄍㄨㄢˇ | (N) | tea house |
| 13 | 決定 | juédìng | ㄐㄩㄝˊ ㄉㄧㄥˋ | (Vp) | to decide |
| 14 | 要是 | yàoshì | ㄧㄠˋ ㄕˋ | (Conj) | if |
| 15 | 就 | jiù | ㄐㄧㄡˋ | (Adv) | then |

## Names

| 16 | 貓空 | Māokōng | ㄇㄠ ㄎㄨㄥ | | Maokong, name of a must-see place in Taipei to visit for fine tea and scenery |
|---|---|---|---|---|---|

## 文法 Grammar

### I. Time-When vs. Time-Duration  09-05

**Function:** Time-When expressions are words or phrases that indicate when an action takes place or a situation happens. They refer to a point in time, e.g., 6:30 this morning. Time-Duration expressions refer to a stretch of time, e.g., 2 hours. See examples below.

Time-When

|         | Past        | Present     | Future      |
|---------|-------------|-------------|-------------|
| **Year**  | 去年        | 今年        | 明年        |
| **Month** | 上個月      | 這個月      | 下個月      |
| **Week**  | 上個星期／禮拜 | 這個星期／禮拜 | 下個星期／禮拜 |
| **Day**   | 昨天        | 今天        | 明天        |

註：年 *nián*, year；禮拜 *lǐbài*, week。

Time-When vs. Time-Duration

|         | Time-When                     | Time-Duration                        |
|---------|-------------------------------|--------------------------------------|
| **Year**  | 2013 年、2014 年、2015 年…    | 一年、兩年、三年…<br>半年、一年半        |
| **Month** | 一月、二月、三月…             | 一個月、兩個月、三個月…<br>半個月、一個半月 |
| **Week**  | 星期一、星期二…<br>星期日／天  | 一個星期、兩個星期…                   |
| **Day**   | 1 日（號）、2 日、3 日…       | 一天、兩天、三天…<br>半天、一天半        |
| **Hour**  | 一點（鐘）、兩點（鐘）…<br>六點半 | 一個鐘頭、兩個鐘頭…<br>半個鐘頭、六個半鐘頭 |

註：日 *rì*, day。

### 練習 Exercise

Answer the questions below, using either Time-When or Time-Duration expressions.

**1** A：他決定什麼時候到日本去玩？

B：＿＿＿＿＿＿＿＿＿＿＿＿＿＿＿＿＿＿。（下個月）

**2** A：你打算學多久（的）中文？

B：＿＿＿＿＿＿＿＿＿＿＿＿＿＿＿＿＿。（五年）

**3** A：你什麼時候回國？

B：＿＿＿＿＿＿＿＿＿＿＿＿＿＿＿＿＿。（下個星期二）

## II. Time-Duration '*for a period of time*'    09-06

**Function:** Time-Duration expressions indicate the length of time, i.e., 'how long', an action takes.

**1** 我去花蓮玩一個星期。

**2** 這個電影很有意思，可是要看三個鐘頭。

**3** 中文，我想學一年半。

### Structures:

1. Duration expressions follow the verb directly, i.e, Subject + Verb + duration.

   **(1)** 我去日本旅行一個多星期。

   **(2)** 這麼多甜點，我們要吃一個星期。

   **(3)** 我想坐高鐵去臺南玩兩天。

   **(4)** 中文課，我們學校要上四年。

2. If the verb has an object, you must repeat the verb:
   Subject + Verb + Object + Verb + duration.

   **(1)** 他打算教中文教一年。

   **(2)** 我每個星期學書法學兩天。

   **(3)** 今年我想在臺灣學中文學九個月。

3. Time-Duration is placed in front of negation.

**(1)** 他太忙了，所以他兩天不能來上課。

**(2)** 這裡沒有網路，所以我兩個星期不能上網。

**(3)** 她要回美國，所以一個月不能上課。

4. When a separable verb takes Time-Duration, the time expression is inserted into the separable verb, either with or without 的.

**(1)** 我每星期上五天的課。

**(2)** 學校下個月放三天的假。

**(3)** 我們打算明天去 KTV 唱三個鐘頭的歌。

**(4)** 你決定在臺灣學多久的中文？

**練習 Exercise**

Please use the "V+time-duration" pattern to talk about Antong's daily activities using the schedule below, e.g., 他早上上一個鐘頭的網。

## —Antong's Day—

**III.** …的時候 de shíhòu   *when*    09-07

拼音、英譯 p.93

**Function:** The '…的時候…' pattern indicates the time an event takes, took, or will take place.

**❶** 在山上看風景的時候，我覺得很舒服。

**❷** 放假的時候，我喜歡去逛夜市。

**❸** 你有空的時候，請到我家來玩。

### 練習 **Exercise**

Answer the questions below using the 的時候 pattern. Base your answers on the pictures.

**❶**

有空的時候，你喜歡做什麼？
（跟朋友一起…）

**❷**

放假的時候，你要做什麼？

**❸**

不上課的時候，你想做什麼？

**❹**

週末的時候，你常做什麼？

**IV.** 有時候 yǒu shíhòu…，有時候 yǒu shíhòu…   *sometimes…, and sometimes…*

 09-08

拼音、英譯 p.93

**Function:** The 有時候…，有時候… refers to two alternating possibilities of events within a given situation.

❶ 我有時候吃中國菜，有時候吃越南菜。
❷ 在圖書館的時候，我有時候看書，有時候上網。
❸ 放假的時候，我有時候在家寫功課，有時候出去玩。

**練習 Exercise**

Pair up to do Q and A. Then find out which activities your classmates do most frequently.

| | Q（問） | A（答） |
|---|---|---|
| 1 | 在家的時候，你做什麼？ | 有時候寫功課，有時候看電視。 |
| 2 | 週末的時候，你做什麼？ | 有時候＿＿＿＿＿＿＿＿＿＿，<br>有時候＿＿＿＿＿＿＿＿＿＿。 |
| 3 | 有空的時候，你做什麼？ | 有時候＿＿＿＿＿＿＿＿＿＿，<br>有時候＿＿＿＿＿＿＿＿＿＿。 |
| 4 | 放假的時候，你做什麼？ | 有時候＿＿＿＿＿＿＿＿＿＿，<br>有時候＿＿＿＿＿＿＿＿＿＿。 |
| 5 | 在餐廳吃飯的時候，你吃什麼？ | 有時候吃＿＿＿＿＿＿＿＿＿，<br>有時候吃＿＿＿＿＿＿＿＿＿。 |

## V. Condition and Consequence with 要是 yàoshì…就 jiù…

拼音、英譯 p.93

09-09

**Function:** In this pattern, 要是 presents the condition, while 就 in the second clause presents the consequence.

❶ 要是我有錢，我就買大房子。
❷ 我要是不回國，我就跟你們一起去玩。
❸ 要是我有空，我就跟朋友一起去 KTV 唱歌。

**Structures:** 要是 *yàoshì* is a conjunction, which can be placed before or after the subject of the first clause. In the second clause, 就 is an adverb and is placed at the very beginning of the predicate.

**❶** 你要是星期日有空，你就跟我去旅行吧！

**❷** 要是下個月不忙，她就回國。

**❸** 你要是沒空，我們就不要去逛夜市。

## 練習 Exercise

Answer the following questions by presenting conditions in the first clauses.

| | Q（問） | A（答） |
|---|---|---|
| 1 | 明天去看電影嗎？ | 要是 ＿＿＿＿＿＿＿＿， 我就 ＿＿＿＿＿＿＿＿。 |
| 2 | 這個週末，你要來我家嗎？ | ＿＿＿＿＿＿＿＿， ＿＿＿＿＿＿＿＿。 |
| 3 | 星期六你要跟我去看籃球比賽嗎？ | ＿＿＿＿＿＿＿＿， ＿＿＿＿＿＿＿＿。 |
| 4 | 今天下課，你去不去圖書館看書？ | ＿＿＿＿＿＿＿＿， ＿＿＿＿＿＿＿＿。 |
| 5 | 你想去貓空喝茶嗎？ | ＿＿＿＿＿＿＿＿， ＿＿＿＿＿＿＿＿。 |

## 語法例句拼音與英譯
## Grammar Examples in Pinyin and English

## II. Time-Duration *'for a period of time'*

### Function:

1. Wǒ qù Huālián wán yí ge xīngqí.
2. Zhè ge diànyǐng hěn yǒu yìsī, kěshì yào kàn sān ge zhōngtóu.
3. Zhōngwén, wǒ xiǎng xué yì nián bàn.

### Function:

1. I'll be in Hualien for a week.
2. This movie is interesting, but you have to watch it for three hours.
3. I'd like to study Chinese for one and a half years.

### Structures:

1. (1) Wǒ qù Rìběn lǚxíng yí ge duō xīngqí.

   (2) Zhème duō tiándiǎn, wǒmen yào chī yí ge xīngqí.

   (3) Wǒ xiǎng zuò gāotiě qù Táinán wán liǎng tiān.

   (4) Zhōngwén kè, wǒmen xuéxiào yào shàng sì nián.

2. (1) Tā dǎsuàn jiāo Zhōngwén jiāo yì nián.
   (2) Wǒ měi ge xīngqí xué shūfǎ xué liǎng tiān.
   (3) Jīnnián wǒ xiǎng zài Táiwān xué Zhōngwén xué jiǔ ge yuè.

3. (1) Tā tài máng le, suǒyǐ tā liǎng tiān bù néng lái shàngkè.
   (2) Zhèlǐ méi yǒu wǎnglù, suǒyǐ wǒ liǎng ge xīngqí bù néng shàngwǎng.
   (3) Tā yào huí Měiguó, suǒyǐ yí ge yuè bù néng shàngkè.

4. (1) Wǒ měi xīngqí shàng wǔ tiān de kè.
   (2) Xuéxiào xià ge yuè fàng sān tiān de jià.
   (3) Wǒmen dǎsuàn míngtiān qù KTV chàng sān ge zhōngtóu de gē.
   (4) Nǐ juédìng zài Táiwān xué duō jiǔ de Zhōngwén?

### Structures:

1. (1) I went to Japan to travel for a little over a week.
   (2) So many desserts! It'll take us a week to eat (it all).
   (3) I would like to take the HSR and kick around in Tainan for two days.
   (4) We need to take Chinese classes for four years at our school.

2. (1) He wants to teach Chinese for a year.
   (2) I study calligraphy two days every week.
   (3) This year, I would like to study Chinese in Taiwan for nine months.

3. (1) He was too busy, so he did not come to class for two days.
   (2) There is no internet here, so I can't go online for two weeks.
   (3) She is returning to the US, so she will not be coming to class for a month.

4. (1) I have classes five days a week.
   (2) Our school has three-days off next month.
   (3) We plan to go to KTV tomorrow to sing for three hours.
   (4) How long did you decide to study Chinese in Taiwan?

## III. ···的時候 de shíhòu  *when*

### Function:

❶ Zài shānshàng kàn fēngjǐng de shíhòu, wǒ juéde hěn shūfú.

❷ Fàngjià de shíhòu, wǒ xǐhuān qù guàng yèshì.

❸ Nǐ yǒu kòng de shíhòu, qǐng dào wǒ jiā lái wán.

### Function:

❶ I felt great when I was on the mountain looking at the scenery.

❷ I like visiting night markets on days off.

❸ When you have time, please come to my place.

## IV. 有時候 yǒu shíhòu··· ，有時候 yǒu shíhòu···  *sometimes..., and sometimes...*

### Function:

❶ Wǒ yǒu shíhòu chī Zhōngguó cài, yǒu shíhòu chī Yuènán cài.

❷ Zài túshūguǎn de shíhòu, wǒ yǒu shíhòu kànshū, yǒu shíhòu shàngwǎng.

❸ Fàngjià de shíhòu, wǒ yǒu shíhòu zài jiā xiě gōngkè, yǒu shíhòu chūqù wán.

### Function:

❶ Sometimes I eat Chinese food, and sometimes I eat Vietnamese food.

❷ When I am in the library, sometimes I read, sometimes I use the internet.

❸ During days off, sometimes I stay home and do homework, sometimes I go out and enjoy myself.

## V. Condition and Consequence with 要是 yàoshì···就 jiù···

### Function:

❶ Yàoshì wǒ yǒu qián, wǒ jiù mǎi dà fángzi.

❷ Wǒ yàoshì bù huíguó, wǒ jiù gēn nǐmen yìqǐ qù wán.

❸ Yàoshì wǒ yǒu kòng, wǒ jiù gēn péngyǒu yìqǐ qù KTV chànggē.

### Function:

❶ If I were rich, I would buy a big house.

❷ If I do not go back to my country, I will go out with you.

❸ If I am free, I will go sing with friends at a KTV.

### Structures:

❶ Nǐ yàoshì xīngqírì yǒu kòng, nǐ jiù gēn wǒ qù lǚxíng ba!

❷ Yàoshì xià ge yuè bù máng, tā jiù huíguó.

❸ Nǐ yàoshì méi kòng, wǒmen jiù bú yào qù guàng yèshì.

### Structures:

❶ If you are free on Sunday, go with me on a trip.

❷ If she is not busy next month, she will return to her country.

❸ If you are not free, we will not go to the night market.

## 課 室 活 動 Classroom Activities

### I. How Much Time Is Spent?

**Goal:** Learning to use time expressions to describe events.

**Task:** Look at the information below and tell the class how much time was spent on each activity.

**❶** 田中想去花蓮玩幾天？

**❷** 安同打算在臺灣學多久的中文？

**❸** 月美跟臺灣朋友打算去貓空玩多久？

**❹** 如玉的爸媽決定在臺灣旅行多久？

## II. Giving Suggestions

**Goal:** Learning to discuss hypothetical situations.

**Task:** Your friend doesn't always like the advice you give. What other suggestions can you give him? Talk with a classmate and see if he/she has any other suggestions.

Example

要是你不喜歡喝咖啡，就喝茶。

| | Example<br>不喜歡… | 1.<br>不要… | 2.<br>不想… |
|---|---|---|---|
| ✗ | | | |
| ✓ | | | |

| | 3.<br>不去… | 4.<br>不喜歡… | 5.<br>覺得…沒意思 |
|---|---|---|---|
| ✗ | | | |
| ✓ | | | |

### III. Traveling Plans

**Goal:** Learning to discuss travel plans with friends.

**Task 1:** A friend of 安同 Antong is visiting from the US. Please tell the class of his plans to travel to 花蓮 Hualien.

| | |
|---|---|
| 星期五 | 14:00　坐火車（從臺北到花蓮） |
| | 18:00　吃晚飯（花蓮的日日好餐廳） |
| | 20:00　去逛夜市 |
| 星期六 | 8:00～16:00 在太魯閣（Tàilǔgé, Taroko Gorge） |
| | 16:30　去參觀大學 |
| | 19:00　吃有名的小吃 |
| 星期日 | 7:30　吃早餐 |
| | 9:00　坐火車（從花蓮回臺北車站） |
| | 12:30　坐計程車回宿舍 |

**Task 2:** Pair up with someone and ask each other about their plans for the upcoming vacation. Where are they going? With whom? How are they planning on getting there? How long do they plan to be away? Write the answers in the table below and compare which place is more popular.

| 同學名字<br>Name of classmates | 去哪裡？<br>Where to? | 跟誰？<br>Whom with? | 怎麼去？<br>How to get there? | 去多久？<br>For how long? |
|---|---|---|---|---|
| | | | | |
| | | | | |
| | | | | |
| | | | | |

最多人去 _____。

## 文化 *Bits of Chinese Culture*

## Subtitled Television Programs

With the exception to news, all television programs in Taiwan come with subtitles and there is no option to remove them. Taiwanese are accustomed to watching television or movies with subtitles, which make comprehending programs easier. There are a few general explanations as to why programs come with subtitles. One understanding is that with the subtitles, the hearing-impaired can also understand programs. Another explanation is that since there are many dialects spoken in Taiwan and accents in Mandarin vary among people and places, subtitles help people understand the programs better as the written language is the same across all Chinese dialects. The third rationale is that since Chinese is a tonal language with different tones having different meanings, when words are placed together, their tones can be affected. Therefore, it is very likely that words with the same sounds can cause misinterpretation.

Furthermore, Chinese is not an alphabetic language and the connection between words and sounds is not as strong. Visualizing the words and hearing the sounds make it easier to understand what is being said. For example, if one hears the phrase "基隆是雨港" *Jīlóng shì yǔ gǎng.* (Keelung is a rainy seaport) without seeing the characters, it is possible that the phrase could be understood as "基隆是漁港" *Jīlóng shì yú gǎng.* (Keelung is a fishing port). With subtitles, misunderstandings like these can be eliminated.

▲ TV shows with subtitles

節目畫面提供：udn TV

97

## Self-Assessment Checklist

I can use time expressions to describe events.

20%      40%      60%      80%      100%

I can discuss travel plans with friends.

20%      40%      60%      80%      100%

I can talk about hypothetical situations.

20%      40%      60%      80%      100%

I can give suggestions about leisure activities.

20%      40%      60%      80%      100%

# LESSON 10

## 第十課

## 臺灣的水果很好吃
### The Fruit in Taiwan Tastes Really Good

**學習目標 Learning Objectives**

**Topic:** 人或物件外貌
**The Appearance of People and Things**

- Learning to give simple descriptions of someone's appearance.
- Learning to describe the color, smell, and taste of food.
- Learning to briefly explain and give reasons.
- Learning to describe tentative activities and changeable states.

# 臺灣的水果很好吃

## The Fruit in Taiwan Tastes Really Good

對話一 Dialogue 1  🎧 10-01  AR 10-A

如　玉：這個黃色的水果叫什麼？

月　美：芒果。給妳一塊，吃吃看。

如　玉：好，謝謝。**[taking a bite]** 香香的、甜甜的，很好吃。

月　美：昨天明華給我們的那種水果，紅色的，叫什麼？

如　玉：妳說的是西瓜吧？

月　美：對！對！對！臺灣有很多好吃的水果。

如　玉：我以前不喜歡吃水果，現在很喜歡了。

月　美：越南的水果也很好吃。

如　玉：要是有機會，我想吃吃看。

月　美：妳來越南，我一定請妳吃。

## 課文拼音 Text in Pinyin

| Rúyù | : Zhè ge huángsè de shuǐguǒ jiào shénme? |
|---|---|
| Yuèměi | : Mángguǒ. Gěi nǐ yí kuài, chīchīkàn. |
| Rúyù | : Hǎo, xièxie. Xiāngxiāng de, tiántián de, hěn hǎochī. |
| Yuèměi | : Zuótiān Mínghuá gěi wǒmen de nà zhǒng shuǐguǒ, hóngsè de, jiào shénme? |
| Rúyù | : Nǐ shuō de shì xīguā ba? |
| Yuèměi | : Duì! Duì! Duì! Táiwān yǒu hěn duō hǎochī de shuǐguǒ. |
| Rúyù | : Wǒ yǐqián bù xǐhuān chī shuǐguǒ, xiànzài hěn xǐhuān le. |
| Yuèměi | : Yuènán de shuǐguǒ yě hěn hǎochī. |
| Rúyù | : Yàoshì yǒu jīhuì, wǒ xiǎng chīchīkàn. |
| Yuèměi | : Nǐ lái Yuènán, wǒ yídìng qǐng nǐ chī. |

## 課文英譯 Text in English

| Ruyu | : What is this yellow fruit called? |
|---|---|
| Yuemei | : Mango. Let me give you a piece. Try it. |
| Ruyu | : OK. Thank you. It is fragrant and sweet. It tastes good. |
| Yuemei | : What is that fruit, the red one, that Minghua gave us yesterday called? |
| Ruyu | : I think you mean the watermelon. |
| Yuemei | : Yes! That's right! Taiwan has a lot of delicious fruits. |
| Ruyu | : In the past, I didn't like to eat fruit, but now, I like it very much. |
| Yuemei | : Fruit in Vietnam is very good, too. |
| Ruyu | : If I get the opportunity, I'd like to try it. |
| Yuemei | : If you come to Vietnam, I will treat you to some. |

## 生詞一 Vocabulary 1 🎧 10-02

### Vocabulary

| | | | | | |
|---|---|---|---|---|---|
| 1 | 水果 | shuǐguǒ | ㄕㄨˇ ㄍㄨㄛˇ | (N) | fruit |
| 2 | 黃色 | huángsè | ㄏㄨㄤˊ ㄙㄜˋ | (N) | yellow |
| 3 | 芒果 | mángguǒ | ㄇㄤˊ ㄍㄨㄛˇ | (N) | mango |
| 4 | 給 | gěi | ㄍㄟˇ | (V) | to give |
| 5 | 塊 | kuài | ㄎㄨㄞˋ | (M) | measure word for pieces of food (e.g., meat, cake) |
| 6 | 香 | xiāng | ㄒㄧㄤ | (Vs) | fragrant |
| 7 | 甜 | tián | ㄊㄧㄢˊ | (Vs) | sweet (taste) |
| 8 | 紅色 | hóngsè | ㄏㄨㄥˊ ㄙㄜˋ | (N) | red |
| 9 | 西瓜 | xīguā | ㄒㄧ ㄍㄨㄚ | (N) | watermelon |
| 10 | 吧 | ba | ㄅㄚ | (Ptc) | sentence-final particle for guessing |
| 11 | 對 | duì | ㄉㄨㄟˋ | (Vs) | correct, right |
| 12 | 以前 | yǐqián | ㄧˇ ㄑㄧㄢˊ | (N) | before |
| 13 | 機會 | jīhuì | ㄐㄧ ㄏㄨㄟˋ | (N) | opportunity |
| 14 | 請 | qǐng | ㄑㄧㄥˇ | (V) | to treat sb to sth |

### Phrases

| | | | | | |
|---|---|---|---|---|---|
| 15 | 吃吃看 | chīchīkàn | ㄔ ㄔ ㄎㄢˋ | | to have a taste, try it, taste it |

對話二 Dialogue 2  10-03  10-B

明　華：你跟你女朋友上個月去花蓮玩，好玩嗎？

田　中：很好玩。你看，這些是我拍的照片。

明　華：你們笑得很開心！哪一個是你女朋友？

田　中：穿紅衣服的這個。穿黃衣服的是旅館老闆的
　　　　太太。

明　華：她們兩個都很漂亮。這兩個男的是誰？

田　中：矮的是旅館的老闆，高的是他弟弟。

明　華：那家旅館怎麼樣？

田　中：很乾淨。從窗戶往外看，是藍色的大海。

明　華：真不錯！那家旅館貴嗎？

田　中：因為現在去玩的人比較少，所以旅館不太貴。

明　華：下次我也想去住。

## 课文拼音 Text in Pinyin

| | |
|---|---|
| Mínghuá | : Nǐ gēn nǐ nǚ péngyǒu shàng ge yuè qù Huālián wán, hǎowán ma? |
| Tiánzhōng | : Hěn hǎowán. Nǐ kàn, zhèxiē shì wǒ pāi de zhàopiàn. |
| Mínghuá | : Nǐmen xiào de hěn kāixīn! Nǎ yí ge shì nǐ nǚ péngyǒu? |
| Tiánzhōng | : Chuān hóng yīfú de zhè ge. Chuān huáng yīfú de shì lǚguǎn lǎobǎn de tàitai. |
| Mínghuá | : Tāmen liǎng ge dōu hěn piàoliàng. Zhè liǎng ge nán de shì shéi? |
| Tiánzhōng | : Ǎi de shì lǚguǎn de lǎobǎn, gāo de shì tā dìdi. |
| Mínghuá | : Nà jiā lǚguǎn zěnmeyàng? |
| Tiánzhōng | : Hěn gānjìng. Cóng chuānghù wǎng wài kàn, shì lánsè de dàhǎi. |
| Mínghuá | : Zhēn búcuò! Nà jiā lǚguǎn guì ma? |
| Tiánzhōng | : Yīnwèi xiànzài qù wán de rén bǐjiào shǎo, suǒyǐ lǚguǎn bú tài guì. |
| Mínghuá | : Xià cì wǒ yě xiǎng qù zhù. |

## 課文英譯 Text in English

| | |
|---|---|
| Minghua | : Did you have a good time with your girlfriend in Hualien last month? |
| Tianzhong | : Yes. Look. I took these pictures. |
| Minghua | : You are smiling from ear to ear. Which one is your girlfriend? |
| Tianzhong | : This one wearing red. The one in yellow is the wife of the owner of the hotel. |
| Minghua | : They are both pretty. Who are these two men? |
| Tianzhong | : The shorter one is the owner of the hotel and the taller one is his younger brother. |
| Minghua | : How was the hotel? |
| Tianzhong | : It was very clean. Looking out from the windows, you could see the blue ocean. |
| Minghua | : That's really nice. Was that hotel expensive? |
| Tianzhong | : Fewer people are going there now, so the hotel wasn't too expensive. |
| Minghua | : I'd also like to stay there next time. |

## 生詞二 Vocabulary 2  🎧 10-04

### Vocabulary

| 1 | 拍 | pāi | ㄆㄞ | (V) | to take (pictures) |
|---|---|---|---|---|---|
| 2 | 笑 | xiào | ㄒㄧㄠ | (V) | to laugh, to smile |
| 3 | 開心 | kāixīn | ㄎㄞ ㄒㄧㄣ | (Vs) | happy |
| 4 | 穿 | chuān | ㄔㄨㄢ | (V) | to wear, to put on |
| 5 | 衣服 | yīfú | ㄧ ㄈㄨˊ | (N) | clothes |
| 6 | 旅館 | lǚguǎn | ㄌㄩˇ ㄍㄨㄢˇ | (N) | hotel |
| 7 | 太太 | tàitai | ㄊㄞˋ ㄊㄞ | (N) | wife |
| 8 | 男 + noun | nán | ㄋㄢˊ | (N) | boy-, male- |
| 9 | 矮 | ǎi | ㄞˇ | (Vs) | short (height) |
| 10 | 高 | gāo | ㄍㄠ | (Vs) | tall |
| 11 | 弟弟 | dìdi | ㄉㄧˋ ㄉㄧ | (N) | younger brother |
| 12 | 乾淨 | gānjìng | ㄍㄢ ㄐㄧㄥˋ | (Vs) | clean |
| 13 | 窗戶 | chuānghù | ㄔㄨㄤ ㄏㄨˋ | (N) | window |
| 14 | 往 | wǎng | ㄨㄤˇ | (Prep) | toward, to |
| 15 | 藍色 | lánsè | ㄌㄢˊ ㄙㄜˋ | (N) | blue |
| 16 | 因為 | yīnwèi | ㄧㄣ ㄨㄟˋ | (Conj) | because |
| 17 | 住 | zhù | ㄓㄨˋ | (V) | to stay |

### Phrases

| 18 | 上個月 | shàng ge yuè | ㄕㄤˋ ㄍㄜ ㄩㄝˋ | | last month |
|---|---|---|---|---|---|
| 19 | 這些 | zhèxiē | ㄓㄜˋ ㄒㄧㄝ | | these |

## 文法 Grammar

I. VV 看 kàn *to try and see*  10-05  拼音、英譯 p.112

**Function:** This pattern reduplicates a mono-syllabic action verb and ends with a cognitive verb 看. It suggests "try (verb) and see". Because of the use of 看, the sentence carries a highly tentative tone.

**①** 這杯咖啡很香，你喝喝看。

**②** 聽說你唱歌唱得很好，我想聽聽看。

**③** 那家餐廳的菜很好吃，我想去吃吃看。

**④** 臺灣的夜市很有名，這個週末我想去逛逛看。

**Usage:**

1. In this lesson, we are focusing on a construction in which the reduplication of mono-syllabic verbs is followed by an attempt verb 看. Basic mono-syllabic action verbs can be used in this pattern, e.g., 吃 *chī*, 喝 *hē*, 打 *dǎ*, 寫 *xiě*, 穿 *chuān*, 學 *xué*, 做 *zuò*, 聽 *tīng*, 唱 *chàng*, 逛 *guàng*, 住 *zhù*.

2. This pattern is closely related to the reduplication pattern introduced in Lesson 6. In most circumstances, they are interchangeable, e.g., 這杯咖啡很香，你喝喝看。 vs. 這杯咖啡很香，你喝喝。 "The coffee smells good. Take a sip." However, they are not interchangeable below.

   (1) 我週末常在家看看書、喝喝咖啡、上上網。 "I often spend my weekends reading, drinking coffee, and using the internet." Since the sentence is not used to ask someone to try something, "看" cannot be used.

   (2) Generally speaking, the pattern "VV 看" cannot be followed by an object. You cannot say *喝喝看咖啡. However, the pattern of VV can be followed by an object, such as 吃吃飯、喝喝咖啡、幫幫我.

## 練習 Exercise

Complete the follow sentences using the verbs given below.

吃、喝、學、做、問、打、寫、穿、做、聽

**①** 他做的牛肉湯很香，你 _____。

**②** 我覺得這些音樂很不錯，請你 _____。

**③** 這個甜點很好吃，你要不要 _____？

**④** 書法很美，你想 _____ 嗎？

**⑤** A：有空的時候，我可以去看看你們的書法課嗎？

B：應該可以，可是我得 _____。

## II. Intensification with Reduplicated State Verbs  10-06  拼音、英譯 p.112

**Function:** Reduplication intensifies the tone of a statement, much like the meaning of 很 intensification. It indicates the speaker's subjective feelings, as opposed to objective, factual observation. See the English translation on page 214.

**①** 這碗牛肉湯香香的。　　**②** 熱熱的咖啡，真香。

**③** 那個地方有很多高高的大樓。

### Structures:

1. No degree adverbs can be used with reduplication. For example, one cannot say *這杯茶很香香的 Zhè bēi chá hěn xiāngxiāng de, since both 很 and reduplication intensify.

2. Note that there is a 的 *de* after the reduplicated state verbs. So, it is not *這杯茶香香 Zhè bēi chá xiāngxiāng, but rather 這杯茶香香的。Zhè bēi chá xiāng xiāng de. 'This cup of tea smells good.' When there are two state verbs in a sequence, the first 的 *de* can be omitted. For example, we say 那種水果香香甜甜的。Nà zhǒng shuǐguǒ xiāngxiāng tiántián de. 'That fruit is fragrant and sweet.'

3. Not all state verbs can be reduplicated. For example, those in the right column below cannot be repeated.

| Yes | No |
|---|---|
| 香、甜、高、熱、大 | 多、貴、近 |
| 美、遠、辣、矮 | 忙、新、少 |

**Usage:** Subjective feelings are often expressed in praise or criticism, e.g., when we order coffee, we say 買一杯熱咖啡！and not *買一杯熱熱的咖啡！as ordering is factual, not expressive.

## 練習 Exercise

Describe the pictures using reduplicated state verbs.

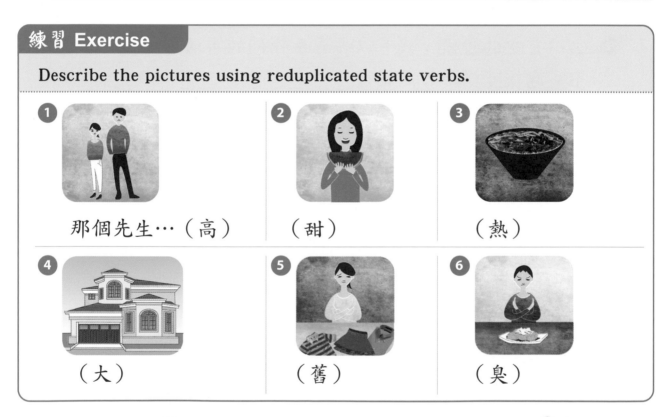

① 那個先生…（高）

② （甜）

③ （熱）

④ （大）

⑤ （舊）

⑥ （臭）

## III. Clause as Modifiers of Nouns  10-07

拼音、英譯 p.112

**Function:** Clauses in Chinese can also be used to modify nouns.

① 你說的水果是西瓜。 ② 他喝的茶是烏龍茶。

③ 這些是我拍的照片。 ④ 穿黃衣服的這個人是老闆。

⑤ 現在去那裡玩的人比較少。 ⑥ 買這種手機的人很多。

**Structures:** Clauses, like all modifiers in Chinese, always precede the nouns they modify. The modification marker 的 *de* comes directly in front of the noun modified. A relative clause itself can be either affirmative, see examples above, or negative, see below.

## ✏️ Negation:

**❶** 不能上網的手機很不方便。

**❷** 不去逛夜市的人可以去茶館喝茶。

**❸** 不來上課的同學不能去看籃球比賽。

**Usage:** Up to this lesson, we have seen that modifiers of nouns include clauses, nouns, adjectives, and verbs. These are all placed in front of the nouns they modify.

## 練習 Exercise

Combine the sentences below into one sentence with a relative clause.

**❶** 他朋友給他一個包子，那個包子很好吃。

→ 他朋友給他的那個包子很好吃。

**❷** 這支手機能上網。這支手機有一點貴。

→ _____

**❸** 這些甜點很香。他做這些甜點。

→ _____

**❹** 他在喝茶。我也喜歡喝那種茶。

→ _____

## IV. Change in Situation with Sentential 了 le  ⌂ 10-08    拼音、英譯 p.113

**Function:** The sentential 了 *le* indicates change in situation, i.e., some change has taken place with a new situation resulting.

❶ 咖啡貴了。

❷ 我會打網球了。

❸ 現在有手機的人多了。

❹ 我現在喜歡吃越南麵了。

**Structures:** The sentential 了 *le* appears at the very end of the sentence, which can be either affirmative or negative.

### ✏ Negation:

❶ 我媽媽不喝咖啡了。

❷ 他不想買那支手機了。

❸ 我們不要去參觀故宮了。

### ✏ Questions:

❶ 你想吃午餐了嗎？

❷ 現在學中文的學生多了嗎？

❸ 你們不去臺東了嗎？

---

### 練習 Exercise

Describe the pictures using the sentential 了 *le.*

❶
我家現在很乾淨了。

❷
車票…（貴）

❸
這個學生…（想學中文）

❹ 這個先生…

## V. Cause and Effect with 因為 *yīnwèi*…，所以 *suǒyǐ*…

 拼音、英譯 p.113

🎧 10-09

**Function:** The '因為 *yīnwèi*…，所以 *suǒyǐ*…' pattern links clauses to indicate cause and effect.

❶ 因為現在去玩的人比較少，所以旅館不太貴。

❷ 因為火車太慢了，所以我想坐高鐵。

❸ 因為我不會做飯，所以常去餐廳吃飯。

❹ 因為我不知道在哪裡買票，所以想請你幫我買。

**Usage:** The two conjuctions, 因為 *yīnwèi* and 所以 *suǒyǐ*, almost always appear as pairs in sentences, while in English, for example, pairing does not happen. Pairing is a reinforcement strategy. In Chinese, cause almost always comes before effect.

### 練習 Exercise

Connect the sentences below using 因為…，所以….

❶ 我很喜歡中國古代的東西。我去參觀故宮。

→ 因為我很喜歡中國古代的東西，所以去參觀故宮。

❷ 我不想買那支手機。那支手機不能照相。

→ _____

❸ 我一定要去看看。我聽說花蓮的風景很美。

→ _____

❹ 我剛開始學中文。我的中文說得不好。

→ _____

語法例句拼音與英譯
**Grammar Examples in Pinyin and English**

## I. V V 看 kàn *to try and see*

**Function:**

❶ Zhè bēi kāfēi hěn xiāng, nǐ hēhēkàn.

❷ Tīngshuō nǐ chàngē chàng de hěn hǎo, wǒ xiǎng tīngtīngkàn.

❸ Nà jiā cāntīng de cài hěn hǎochī, wǒ xiǎng qù chīchīkàn.

❹ Táiwān de yèshì hěn yǒumíng, zhè ge zhōumò wǒ xiǎng qù guàngguàngkàn.

**Function:**

❶ This cup of coffee smells really good. Taste it.

❷ I've heard that you sing well. I'd like to hear.

❸ The food in that restaurant is very good. I'd like to try it and see for myself.

❹ Taiwan's night markets are well known. I'd like to wander around (one) this weekend and see for myself.

## II. Intensification with Reduplicated State Verbs

**Function:**

❶ Zhè wǎn niúròu tāng xiāngxiāng de.

❷ Rèrè de kāfēi, zhēn xiāng.

❸ Nà ge dìfāng yǒu hěn duō gāogāo de dàlóu.

**Function:**

❶ This bowl of beef soup smells really good.

❷ Hot coffee smells really good.

❸ There are many really tall buildings there.

## III. Clause as Modifiers of Nouns

**Function:**

❶ Nǐ shuō de shuǐguǒ shì xīguā.

❷ Tā hē de chá shì Wūlóng chá.

❸ Zhè xiē shì wǒ pāi de zhàopiàn.

❹ Chuān huáng yīfú de zhè ge rén shì lǎobǎn.

❺ Xiànzài qù nàlǐ wán de rén bǐjiào shǎo.

❻ Mǎi zhè zhǒng shǒujī de rén hěn duō.

**Function:**

❶ The fruit you're talking about is watermelon.

❷ The tea he drank was Oolong tea.

❸ These are photos that I took.

❹ The person in a yellow shirt is the (shop) owner.

❺ Now, fewer people are visiting that place.

❻ A lot of people buy this kind of cellphone.

**Structures:**

 **Negation:**

❶ Bù néng shàngwǎng de shǒujī hěn bù fāngbiàn.

❷ Bú qù guàng yèshì de rén kěyǐ qù cháguǎn hē chá.

❸ Bù lái shàngkè de tóngxué bù néng qù kàn lánqiú bǐsài.

**Structures:**

 **Negation:**

❶ Cellphones that cannot go online aren't that useful.

❷ Those who do not want to go to the night market can go drink tea at the tea house.

❸ Students who did not come to class can't go to watch basketall game.

## IV. Change in Situation with Sentential 了 le

### Function:

**1** Kāfēi guì le.

**2** Wǒ huì dǎ wǎngqiú le.

**3** Xiànzài yǒu shǒujī de rén duō le.

**4** Wǒ xiànzài xǐhuān chī Yuènán miàn le.

### Structures:

### ✎ Negation:

**1** Wǒ māma bù hē kāfēi le.

**2** Tā bù xiǎng mǎi nà zhī shǒujī le.

**3** Wǒmen bú yào qù cānguān Gùgōng le.

### ✎ Questions:

**1** Nǐ xiǎng chī wǔcān le ma?

**2** Xiànzài xué Zhōngwén de xuéshēng duō le ma?

**3** Nǐmen bú qù Táidōng le ma?

### Function:

**1** Coffee is more expensive than before.

**2** I know how to play tennis now. (I didn't before.)

**3** More people own cellphones now.

**4** I've come to like Vietnamese noodles. (I didn't before.)

### Structures:

### ✎ Negation:

**1** My mom doesn't drink coffee any more.

**2** He doesn't want to buy that cellphone any more.

**3** We don't want to visit the Palace Museum any more.

### ✎ Questions:

**1** Do you want to eat lunch now?

**2** Are more students studying Chinese now?

**3** You're not going to Taitung?

## V. Cause and Effect with 因為 yīnwèi… ，所以 suǒyǐ…

### Function:

**1** Yīnwèi xiànzài qù wán de rén bǐjiào shǎo, suǒyǐ lǚguǎn bú tài guì.

**2** Yīnwèi huǒchē tài màn le, suǒyǐ wǒ xiǎng zuò gāotiě.

**3** Yīnwèi wǒ bú huì zuòfàn, suǒyǐ cháng qù cāntīng chīfàn.

**4** Yīnwèi wǒ bù zhīdào zài nǎlǐ mǎi piào, suǒyǐ xiǎng qǐng nǐ bāng wǒ mǎi.

### Function:

**1** Because now fewer people go there, (therefore) the hotels are not that expensive.

**2** Because the train is too slow, so I'd like to take the HSR.

**3** Because I don't know how to cook, (therefore) (I) often go to eat at restaurants.

**4** Because I don't know where to buy tickets, (so) (I)'d like to ask you to buy one for me.

課 室 活 動 **Classroom Activities**

## I. Which One Do You Prefer?

**Goals:** Learning to give simple descriptions of someone's appearance. Learning to describe the color, smell, and taste of food.

**Task 1:** Pair up with someone. Take a look at the pictures below. Tell your partner which you prefer and why.

❶ 哪一個人比較好看？

❷ 哪一張照片比較漂亮？

A      B

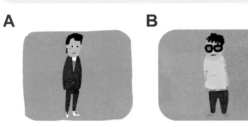

A      B

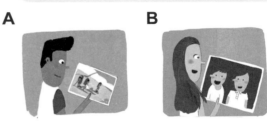

❸ 你想看哪一個電影？

❹ 你比較想去哪一個海邊玩？

A      B

    馬安同      田中誠一

A      B

❺ 你比較想去哪一家餐廳吃飯？

❻ 你比較喜歡吃哪一種西瓜？

A      B

    小籠包店      牛肉麵店

A      B

LESSON •10• 臺灣的水果很好吃

**The Fruit in Taiwan Tastes Really Good**

**7** 你比較喜歡喝哪一種咖啡？

A   B

**8** 你比較喜歡穿什麼衣服？

A   B

**9** 你比較想住哪一個地方？

A   B

**Task 2:** Tell the class what your choices are and tally others' choices using 「正」。 （一 丁 下 正 正）

|   | 1 | 2 | 3 | 4 | 5 | 6 | 7 | 8 | 9 |
|---|---|---|---|---|---|---|---|---|---|
| A |   |   |   |   |   |   |   |   |   |
| B |   |   |   |   |   |   |   |   |   |

## II. Then and Now

**Goal:** Learning to describe changes in situation.

**Task 1:** Ask your classmates if they have made any changes since they arrived in Taiwan. Also, have there been any changes in their countries between now and the past? Write down your classmates' names if the answers are in the affirmative.

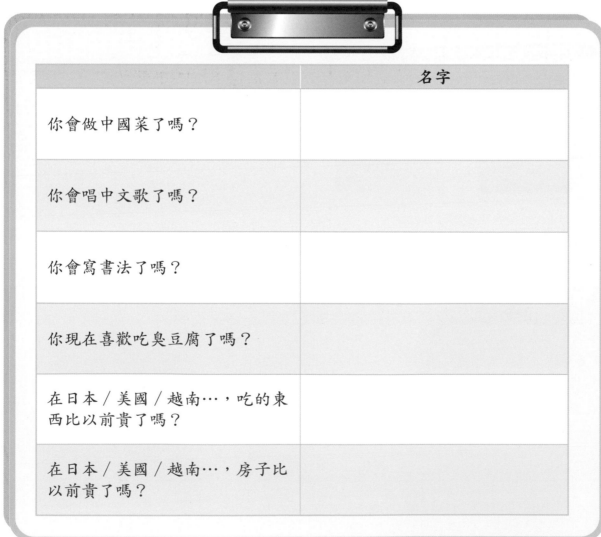

| | 名字 |
|---|---|
| 你會做中國菜了嗎？ | |
| 你會唱中文歌了嗎？ | |
| 你會寫書法了嗎？ | |
| 你現在喜歡吃臭豆腐了嗎？ | |
| 在日本／美國／越南…，吃的東西比以前貴了嗎？ | |
| 在日本／美國／越南…，房子比以前貴了嗎？ | |

**Task 2:** Think about at least two things that have changed in your, your friend's, or your friends's situations. Share them with the class.

1. _____

2. _____

## III. Your Observations on Taiwanese Society

**Goal:** Learning to briefly explain and give reasons.
**Task:** Pair up with someone and hold discussions based on the following five questions. Share your conclusions with the class.

❶ 為什麼很多人到臺灣來學中文？

❷ 為什麼現在學中文的人比以前多？

❸ 在臺灣，為什麼很多人不常在家吃飯？

❹ 在臺灣，為什麼很多人喜歡去夜市？

❺ 在臺灣，為什麼很多人騎機車？

## 文化 *Bits of Chinese Culture*

# The Meanings of Different Colors

In Chinese culture, it is important that you understand that three colors have significant meanings. They are red, white, and yellow.

Red is an auspicioius color used for happy events. In traditional Chinese weddings, all wedding garments and decorations are red. Wedding guests bring red envelopes with money in them for the newlyweds to bring them good luck. During Chinese New Year, people hang up red New Year's scrolls and couplets and the character 福 *fú* (blessing) is also written on red paper to bring good luck. Adults give children money-stuffed red envelopes.

▲ Traditional red Chinese wedding garments

▲ White wedding gown

▲ Red envelopes　　▲ White envelopes

▲ Traditional white Japanese wedding gown

▲ Red New Year scrolls
蕙風堂／提供

While red is for joy and birth, white is for death. Clothing worn by family members at funerals is white and items at funerals services are covered in white. People paying their respects at funerals offer a white envelope to the mourning family. However, with the influence of western culture, brides are now wearing white wedding dresses. In the West and in Japan, white signifies pureness. In Chinese culture, white has also come to mean pure.

▲ The traditional royal color—yellow
《中國顏色》黃仁達／著作、提供

The last important color is yellow. The meaning of yellow has changed dramatically since ancient times. In imperial China, yellow was used exclusively by the emperor and the royal family. It was the color of the highest class. The robe worn by the emperor was called 黃袍 *huángpáo* (literally "yellow gown"). Emperors and royal families no longer exist in modern China and the significance of the color yellow has undergone dramatic change. Today, it can mean "pornography" with the term 黃色書刊 *huángsè shūkān* meaning "pornographic books".

## Self-Assessment Checklist

I can give simple descriptions of a person's appearance.

20%　　40%　　60%　　80%　　100%

I can describe the color, smell, and taste of food.

20%　　40%　　60%　　80%　　100%

I can briefly explain and give reasons.

20%　　40%　　60%　　80%　　100%

I can describe tentative activities and changes in situations.

20%　　40%　　60%　　80%　　100%

| Pinyin | Traditional Characters | Simplified Characters | Lesson-Dialogue-Number |
|---|---|---|---|
| **A** | | | |
| a | 啊 | 啊 | 3-1-21 |
| a | 啊 | 啊 | 13-1-4 |
| ǎi | 矮 | 矮 | 10-2-9 |
| **B** | | | |
| ba | 吧 | 吧 | 3-2-9 |
| ba | 吧 | 吧 | 10-1-10 |
| bǎ | 把 | 把 | 15-1-17 |
| bàba | 爸爸 | 爸爸 | 2-1-20 |
| bǎi | 百 | 百 | 4-1-15 |
| Bái Rúyù | 白如玉 | 白如玉 | 3-2-1 |
| bàn | 半 | 半 | 7-2-6 |
| bāng | 幫 | 帮 | 4-1-13 |
| bàngqiú | 棒球 | 棒球 | 3-1-7 |
| bāo | 包 | 包 | 15-2-16 |
| bǎoxiǎn | 保險 | 保险 | 15-2-10 |
| bāozi | 包子 | 包子 | 4-1-8 |
| bēi | 杯 | 杯 | 4-1-6 |
| bǐ | 比 | 比 | 8-2-8 |
| biànlì shāngdiàn | 便利商店 | 便利商店 | 8-1-20 |
| bié | 別 | 别 | 15-2-14 |
| bǐjiào | 比較 | 比较 | 8-1-8 |
| bīng | 冰 | 冰 | 15-2-13 |
| bǐsài | 比賽 | 比赛 | 7-2-7 |
| bíshuǐ | 鼻水 | 鼻水 | 15-1-4 |
| bómǔ | 伯母 | 伯母 | 2-2-2 |
| bù | 不 | 不 | 1-2-11 |
| bù hǎo | 不好 | 不好 | 5-2-17 |
| bù xíng | 不行 | 不行 | 8-2-12 |
| búbì kèqì | 不必客氣 | 不必客气 | 13-1-22 |
| búcuò | 不錯 | 不错 | 5-2-12 |
| búguò | 不過 | 不过 | 11-2-12 |
| bùhǎo yìsi | 不好意思 | 不好意思 | 11-2-15 |
| búkèqì | 不客氣 | 不客气 | 1-1-22 |

| Pinyin | Traditional Characters | Simplified Characters | Lesson-Dialogue-Number |
|---|---|---|---|
| búyòng le | 不用了 | 不用了 | 15-2-20 |
| **C** | | | |
| cài | 菜 | 菜 | 3-2-16 |
| cānguān | 參觀 | 参观 | 8-2-2 |
| cāntīng | 餐廳 | 餐厅 | 5-2-2 |
| chá | 茶 | 茶 | 1-2-3 |
| chā | 差 | 差 | 15-1-8 |
| chābùduō | 差不多 | 差不多 | 8-2-14 |
| cháguǎn | 茶館 | 茶馆 | 9-2-12 |
| cháng | 常 | 常 | 3-1-10 |
| chànggē | 唱歌 | 唱歌 | 7-1-3 |
| chāoshì | 超市 | 超市 | 11-1-8 |
| Chén Yuèměi | 陳月美 | 陈月美 | 1-1-1 |
| chéngjī | 成績 | 成绩 | 12-1-11 |
| chēpiào | 車票 | 车票 | 8-1-10 |
| chī | 吃 | 吃 | 3-2-14 |
| chīchīkàn | 吃吃看 | 吃吃看 | 10-1-15 |
| chīfàn | 吃飯 | 吃饭 | 6-2-10 |
| chòu dòufǔ | 臭豆腐 | 臭豆腐 | 5-1-20 |
| chuān | 穿 | 穿 | 10-2-4 |
| chuānghù | 窗戶 | 窗户 | 10-2-13 |
| chuántǒng | 傳統 | 传统 | 13-2-9 |
| chúfáng | 廚房 | 厨房 | 11-1-4 |
| chūntiān | 春天 | 春天 | 14-1-5 |
| chūqù | 出去 | 出去 | 9-1-8 |
| cì | 次 | 次 | 15-2-6 |
| cóng | 從 | 从 | 7-1-6 |
| **D** | | | |
| dà | 大 | 大 | 4-1-10 |
| dǎ | 打 | 打 | 3-1-5 |
| dà bùfèn | 大部分 | 大部分 | 13-2-15 |
| dǎ diànhuà | 打電話 | 打电话 | 11-1-23 |
| Dà'ān | 大安 | 大安 | 7-1-12 |
| dàgài | 大概 | 大概 | 9-1-9 |

| Pinyin | Traditional Characters | Simplified Characters | Lesson-Dialogue-Number |
|---|---|---|---|
| dài | 帶 | 带 | 9-2-4 |
| dàjiā | 大家 | 大家 | 14-2-10 |
| dàlóu | 大樓 | 大楼 | 6-2-14 |
| dàn | 蛋 | 蛋 | 13-2-7 |
| dàngāo | 蛋糕 | 蛋糕 | 13-2-11 |
| dāngrán | 當然 | 当然 | 13-1-8 |
| dànshì | 但是 | 但是 | 8-1-12 |
| dào | 到 | 到 | 5-2-15 |
| dào | 到 | 到 | 11-1-12 |
| dào | 到 | 到 | 12-1-17 |
| dǎsuàn | 打算 | 打算 | 9-1-3 |
| dàxué | 大學 | 大学 | 12-1-7 |
| de | 的 | 的 | 2-1-3 |
| de | 得 | 得 | 5-2-9 |
| děi | 得 | 得 | 7-1-8 |
| děng | 等 | 等 | 11-2-9 |
| děng yíxià | 等一下 | 等一下 | 7-2-20 |
| diàn | 店 | 店 | 5-1-14 |
| diǎn | 點 | 点 | 5-1-16 |
| diǎn | 點 | 点 | 7-1-1 |
| diànhuà | 電話 | 电话 | 11-1-20 |
| diànshì | 電視 | 电视 | 9-1-4 |
| diànyǐng | 電影 | 电影 | 3-2-5 |
| dìdi | 弟弟 | 弟弟 | 10-2-11 |
| dìfāng | 地方 | 地方 | 6-1-15 |
| dìng | 訂 | 订 | 13-2-3 |
| dòng | 棟 | 栋 | 6-2-13 |
| dōngtiān | 冬天 | 冬天 | 14-1-10 |
| dōngxi | 東西 | 东西 | 6-2-6 |
| dōu | 都 | 都 | 2-1-13 |
| duì | 對 | 对 | 10-1-11 |
| duì | 對 | 对 | 13-2-12 |
| duìbùqǐ | 對不起 | 对不起 | 1-2-18 |
| duìle | 對了 | 对了 | 7-1-15 |
| duō | 多 | 多 | 2-1-11 |
| duō jiǔ | 多久 | 多久 | 9-1-13 |
| duōshǎo | 多少 | 多少 | 4-1-2 |
| dùzi | 肚子 | 肚子 | 15-2-3 |

**F**

| Pinyin | Traditional Characters | Simplified Characters | Lesson-Dialogue-Number |
|---|---|---|---|
| fāngbiàn | 方便 | 方便 | 6-2-2 |
| fángdōng | 房東 | 房东 | 11-1-2 |
| fàngjià | 放假 | 放假 | 9-1-10 |
| fángjiān | 房間 | 房间 | 11-1-15 |
| fángzi | 房子 | 房子 | 2-1-7 |
| fángzū | 房租 | 房租 | 11-2-2 |
| fāshāo | 發燒 | 发烧 | 15-1-12 |
| fāyán | 發炎 | 发炎 | 15-1-10 |
| fēicháng | 非常 | 非常 | 8-1-11 |
| fēn | 分 | 分 | 7-1-4 |
| fēng | 風 | 风 | 14-1-3 |
| fēngjǐng | 風景 | 风景 | 6-1-8 |
| fēnzhōng | 分鐘 | 分钟 | 11-1-10 |
| fù | 付 | 付 | 11-2-13 |
| fùjìn | 附近 | 附近 | 6-1-17 |
| fùmǔ | 父母 | 父母 | 14-1-9 |

**G**

| Pinyin | Traditional Characters | Simplified Characters | Lesson-Dialogue-Number |
|---|---|---|---|
| gāng | 剛 | 刚 | 7-2-3 |
| gānjìng | 乾淨 | 干净 | 10-2-12 |
| gǎnmào | 感冒 | 感冒 | 15-1-13 |
| gāo | 高 | 高 | 10-2-10 |
| gāotiě | 高鐵 | 高铁 | 8-1-18 |
| ge | 個 | 个 | 2-2-10 |
| gēge | 哥哥 | 哥哥 | 2-2-6 |
| gěi | 給 | 给 | 10-1-4 |
| gěi | 給 | 给 | 11-1-21 |
| gēn | 跟 | 跟 | 8-1-3 |
| gēn | 跟 | 跟 | 15-2-11 |
| gèng | 更 | 更 | 14-2-9 |
| gōnggòng qìchē | 公共汽車（公車） | 公共汽车（公车） | 8-2-11 |
| gōngkè | 功課 | 功课 | 9-1-7 |
| gōngsī | 公司 | 公司 | 12-1-13 |
| gōngzuò | 工作 | 工作 | 12-2-1 |
| gōngzuò | 工作 | 工作 | 12-2-8 |
| guàng | 逛 | 逛 | 9-2-10 |

| Pinyin | Traditional Characters | Simplified Characters | Lesson-Dialogue-Number |
|---|---|---|---|
| guānxīn | 關心 | 关心 | 15-2-15 |
| gǔdài | 古代 | 古代 | 8-2-3 |
| Gùgōng Bówùyuàn | 故宮博物院（故宮） | 故宫博物院（故宫） | 8-2-9 |
| guì | 貴 | 贵 | 4-2-11 |
| guò | 過 | 过 | 13-1-15 |
| guójiā | 國家 | 国家 | 12-2-10 |

**H**

| Pinyin | Traditional Characters | Simplified Characters | Lesson-Dialogue-Number |
|---|---|---|---|
| hái | 還 | 还 | 9-2-6 |
| hǎi | 海 | 海 | 6-1-11 |
| háishì | 還是 | 还是 | 3-2-8 |
| hàn | 和 | 和 | 3-1-8 |
| hào | 號 | 号 | 9-2-3 |
| hǎo | 好 | 好 | 1-1-14 |
| hǎo | 好 | 好 | 2-1-9 |
| hǎo | 好 | 好 | 12-2-6 |
| hǎo a | 好啊 | 好啊 | 3-1-23 |
| hǎo bù hǎo | 好不好 | 好不好 | 3-2-18 |
| hǎochī | 好吃 | 好吃 | 5-1-4 |
| hǎode | 好的 | 好的 | 4-1-17 |
| hǎohē | 好喝 | 好喝 | 1-2-5 |
| hǎojiǔ bújiàn | 好久不見 | 好久不见 | 13-1-21 |
| hǎokàn | 好看 | 好看 | 2-1-16 |
| hǎowán | 好玩 | 好玩 | 3-1-16 |
| hǎoxiàng | 好像 | 好像 | 11-2-7 |
| hē | 喝 | 喝 | 1-2-2 |
| hěn | 很 | 很 | 1-2-4 |
| hóngsè | 紅色 | 红色 | 10-1-8 |
| hóngyè | 紅葉 | 红叶 | 14-1-13 |
| hóulóng | 喉嚨 | 喉咙 | 15-1-9 |
| hòumiàn | 後面 | 后面 | 6-1-12 |
| hòutiān | 後天 | 后天 | 7-1-11 |
| huā | 花 | 花 | 12-1-9 |
| Huālián | 花蓮 | 花莲 | 6-1-22 |
| huángsè | 黃色 | 黄色 | 10-1-2 |
| huānyíng | 歡迎 | 欢迎 | 1-1-19 |
| huáxuě | 滑雪 | 滑雪 | 14-1-4 |
| huì | 會 | 会 | 5-2-10 |

| Pinyin | Traditional Characters | Simplified Characters | Lesson-Dialogue-Number |
|---|---|---|---|
| huì | 會 | 会 | 11-2-8 |
| huí jiā | 回家 | 回家 | 15-2-22 |
| huíguó | 回國 | 回国 | 9-1-2 |
| huílái | 回來 | 回来 | 13-1-3 |
| huíqù | 回去 | 回去 | 11-1-17 |
| huǒchē | 火車 | 火车 | 8-1-2 |
| huòshì | 或是 | 或是 | 8-1-16 |

**J**

| Pinyin | Traditional Characters | Simplified Characters | Lesson-Dialogue-Number |
|---|---|---|---|
| jǐ | 幾 | 几 | 2-2-9 |
| jǐ | 幾 | 几 | 15-2-5 |
| jiā | 家 | 家 | 2-1-5 |
| jiā | 家 | 家 | 5-1-13 |
| jiān | 間 | 间 | 11-1-13 |
| jiǎngxuéjīn | 獎學金 | 奖学金 | 12-1-10 |
| jiànkāng | 健康 | 健康 | 15-2-9 |
| jiànkāng zhōngxīn | 健康中心 | 健康中心 | 15-2-21 |
| jiànmiàn | 見面 | 见面 | 7-1-5 |
| jiànyì | 建議 | 建议 | 9-2-7 |
| jiào | 叫 | 叫 | 1-1-16 |
| jiāo | 教 | 教 | 5-2-14 |
| jiāohuàn | 交換 | 交换 | 13-1-10 |
| jiàoshì | 教室 | 教室 | 6-2-17 |
| jiārén | 家人 | 家人 | 2-1-4 |
| jiāyóu | 加油 | 加油 | 12-1-22 |
| jīchē | 機車 | 机车 | 8-2-5 |
| jìchéngchē | 計程車 | 计程车 | 8-2-13 |
| jìde | 記得 | 记得 | 13-1-7 |
| jiē | 接 | 接 | 1-1-9 |
| jiějie | 姐姐 | 姐姐 | 2-1-18 |
| jiěmèi | 姐妹 | 姐妹 | 2-2-13 |
| jiéshù | 結束 | 结束 | 7-2-8 |
| jiéyùn | 捷運 | 捷运 | 8-2-7 |
| jìhuà | 計畫 | 计画 | 12-1-1 |
| jīhuì | 機會 | 机会 | 10-1-13 |
| jìn | 近 | 近 | 6-2-1 |
| jīnnián | 今年 | 今年 | 13-2-2 |
| jīntiān | 今天 | 今天 | 3-2-2 |

| Pinyin | Traditional Characters | Simplified Characters | Lesson-Dialogue-Number |
|---|---|---|---|
| jiù | 舊 | 旧 | 4-2-5 |
| jiù | 就 | 就 | 9-2-15 |
| jiù | 就 | 就 | 11-1-11 |
| jiǔ | 久 | 久 | 12-1-3 |
| juéde | 覺得 | 觉得 | 3-1-15 |
| juédìng | 決定 | 决定 | 9-2-13 |

**K**

| Pinyin | Traditional Characters | Simplified Characters | Lesson-Dialogue-Number |
|---|---|---|---|
| kāfēi | 咖啡 | 咖啡 | 1-2-14 |
| kāishǐ | 開始 | 开始 | 7-2-15 |
| kāixīn | 開心 | 开心 | 10-2-3 |
| kàn | 看 | 看 | 3-2-4 |
| kànbìng | 看病 | 看病 | 15-2-8 |
| kànshū | 看書 | 看书 | 2-2-8 |
| kè | 課 | 课 | 7-2-14 |
| kěpà | 可怕 | 可怕 | 14-2-12 |
| kěshì | 可是 | 可是 | 5-2-3 |
| kètīng | 客廳 | 客厅 | 11-1-3 |
| kěyǐ | 可以 | 可以 | 3-2-10 |
| kěyǐ | 可以 | 可以 | 5-2-13 |
| kěyǐ | 可以 | 可以 | 7-2-18 |
| kōng | 空 | 空 | 11-1-14 |
| kuài | 塊 | 块 | 4-1-16 |
| kuài | 塊 | 快 | 10-1-5 |
| kuài | 快 | 块 | 8-1-9 |
| kuài | 快 | 快 | 14-1-8 |
| kuàilè | 快樂 | 快乐 | 13-1-2 |
| KTV | KTV | KTV | 7-1-2 |

**L**

| Pinyin | Traditional Characters | Simplified Characters | Lesson-Dialogue-Number |
|---|---|---|---|
| là | 辣 | 辣 | 5-2-4 |
| lái | 來 | 来 | 1-1-5 |
| lánqiú | 籃球 | 篮球 | 3-1-11 |
| lánsè | 藍色 | 蓝色 | 10-2-15 |
| lǎobǎn | 老闆 | 老板 | 4-1-4 |
| lǎoshī | 老師 | 老师 | 2-2-7 |
| le | 了 | 了 | 4-2-6 |
| le | 了 | 了 | 13-2-4 |
| lèi | 累 | 累 | 12-1-20 |
| lěng | 冷 | 冷 | 14-1-2 |

| Pinyin | Traditional Characters | Simplified Characters | Lesson-Dialogue-Number |
|---|---|---|---|
| Lǐ Mínghuá | 李明華 | 李明华 | 1-1-2 |
| liǎng | 兩 | 两 | 2-2-15 |
| liǎnsè | 臉色 | 脸色 | 15-2-1 |
| lǐmiàn | 裡面 | 里面 | 6-2-8 |
| Lín | 林 | 林 | 11-1-22 |
| liú | 流 | 流 | 15-1-3 |
| lǐwù | 禮物 | 礼物 | 13-2-1 |
| lóu | 樓 | 楼 | 6-2-12 |
| lóuxià | 樓下 | 楼下 | 6-1-18 |
| lǚguǎn | 旅館 | 旅馆 | 10-2-6 |
| lǚxíng | 旅行 | 旅行 | 9-1-6 |

**M**

| Pinyin | Traditional Characters | Simplified Characters | Lesson-Dialogue-Number |
|---|---|---|---|
| ma | 嗎 | 吗 | 1-1-8 |
| Mǎ Āntóng | 馬安同 | 马安同 | 2-1-2 |
| mài | 賣 | 卖 | 4-2-12 |
| mǎi | 買 | 买 | 4-1-5 |
| māma | 媽媽 | 妈妈 | 2-1-21 |
| màn | 慢 | 慢 | 8-1-6 |
| màn zǒu | 慢走 | 慢走 | 14-2-17 |
| máng | 忙 | 忙 | 7-2-10 |
| mángguǒ | 芒果 | 芒果 | 10-1-3 |
| Māokōng | 貓空 | 猫空 | 9-2-16 |
| méi | 沒 | 没 | 2-2-11 |
| měi | 美 | 美 | 6-1-9 |
| měi | 每 | 每 | 7-2-11 |
| méi guānxi | 沒關係 | 没关系 | 11-2-16 |
| méi wèntí | 沒問題 | 没问题 | 7-1-14 |
| Měiguó | 美國 | 美国 | 1-2-17 |
| mèimei | 妹妹 | 妹妹 | 2-1-19 |
| ménkǒu | 門口 | 门口 | 13-1-17 |
| miàn | 麵 | 面 | 5-1-2 |
| miànxiàn | 麵線 | 面线 | 13-2-6 |
| míngnián | 明年 | 明年 | 14-1-11 |
| míngtiān | 明天 | 明天 | 3-1-17 |
| míngzi | 名字 | 名字 | 2-2-4 |

**N**

| Pinyin | Traditional Characters | Simplified Characters | Lesson-Dialogue-Number |
|---|---|---|---|
| ná | 拿 | 拿 | 15-1-16 |
| nà | 那 | 那 | 11-2-10 |

| Pinyin | Traditional Characters | Simplified Characters | Lesson-Dialogue-Number |
|---|---|---|---|
| nà / nèi | 那 | 那 | 4-2-10 |
| nǎ / něi | 哪 | 哪 | 1-2-12 |
| nǎ guó / něi guó | 哪國 | 哪国 | 1-2-19 |
| nàlǐ | 那裡 | 那里 | 6-1-7 |
| nǎlǐ | 哪裡 | 哪里 | 6-1-5 |
| Nǎlǐ, nǎlǐ | 哪裡，哪裡 | 哪里，哪里 | 13-2-14 |
| nàme | 那麼 | 那么 | 12-2-13 |
| nàme | 那麼 | 那么 | 13-1-11 |
| nán | 男 | 男 | 10-2-8 |
| nán | 難 | 难 | 12-2-12 |
| nánkàn | 難看 | 难看 | 15-2-2 |
| ne | 呢 | 呢 | 1-2-9 |
| nèiyòng | 內用 | 内用 | 4-1-19 |
| néng | 能 | 能 | 4-2-8 |
| nǐ | 你 | 你 | 1-1-4 |
| nǐ | 妳 | 妳 | 3-2-6 |
| nǐ hǎo | 你好 | 你好 | 1-1-23 |
| nián | 年 | 年 | 12-1-2 |
| niàn | 念 | 念 | 12-1-6 |
| niánqīng | 年輕 | 年轻 | 13-2-10 |
| niànshū | 念書 | 念书 | 12-1-19 |
| nǐmen | 你們 | 你们 | 1-1-17 |
| nín | 您 | 您 | 2-2-3 |
| niúròu | 牛肉 | 牛肉 | 5-1-1 |
| Niǔyuē | 紐約 | 纽约 | 14-1-16 |
| nǚ | 女 | 女 | 9-2-1 |

**P**

| Pinyin | Traditional Characters | Simplified Characters | Lesson-Dialogue-Number |
|---|---|---|---|
| pà | 怕 | 怕 | 5-2-5 |
| pāi | 拍 | 拍 | 10-2-1 |
| pángbiān | 旁邊 | 旁边 | 6-2-16 |
| péi | 陪 | 陪 | 15-2-7 |
| péngyǒu | 朋友 | 朋友 | 6-1-20 |
| piányí | 便宜 | 便宜 | 4-2-13 |
| piàoliàng | 漂亮 | 漂亮 | 2-1-6 |

**Q**

| Pinyin | Traditional Characters | Simplified Characters | Lesson-Dialogue-Number |
|---|---|---|---|
| qí | 騎 | 骑 | 8-2-4 |
| qián | 錢 | 钱 | 4-1-3 |
| qiān | 千 | 千 | 4-2-16 |

| Pinyin | Traditional Characters | Simplified Characters | Lesson-Dialogue-Number |
|---|---|---|---|
| qiánmiàn | 前面 | 前面 | 6-1-10 |
| qǐng | 請 | 请 | 1-2-1 |
| qǐng | 請 | 请 | 10-1-14 |
| qǐng jìn | 請進 | 请进 | 2-1-22 |
| qǐngwèn | 請問 | 请问 | 1-1-20 |
| qiūtiān | 秋天 | 秋天 | 14-1-12 |
| qù | 去 | 去 | 3-1-19 |
| qùnián | 去年 | 去年 | 12-2-2 |

**R**

| Pinyin | Traditional Characters | Simplified Characters | Lesson-Dialogue-Number |
|---|---|---|---|
| rè | 熱 | 热 | 4-1-7 |
| rén | 人 | 人 | 1-2-7 |
| rèshuǐqì | 熱水器 | 热水器 | 11-2-6 |
| rèxīn | 熱心 | 热心 | 13-1-12 |
| Rìběn | 日本 | 日本 | 1-2-16 |

**S**

| Pinyin | Traditional Characters | Simplified Characters | Lesson-Dialogue-Number |
|---|---|---|---|
| sǎn | 傘 | 伞 | 14-2-2 |
| shān | 山 | 山 | 6-1-13 |
| shàng cì | 上次 | 上次 | 14-2-16 |
| shàng ge yuè | 上個月 | 上个月 | 10-2-18 |
| shàngbān | 上班 | 上班 | 12-1-18 |
| shāngdiàn | 商店 | 商店 | 6-2-9 |
| shàngkè | 上課 | 上课 | 6-1-21 |
| shàngwǎng | 上網 | 上网 | 4-2-9 |
| shānshàng | 山上 | 山上 | 6-1-4 |
| shǎo | 少 | 少 | 5-1-6 |
| shéi | 誰 | 谁 | 2-1-17 |
| shēngbìng | 生病 | 生病 | 15-1-11 |
| shēngrì | 生日 | 生日 | 13-1-1 |
| shēngrì kuàilè | 生日快樂 | 生日快乐 | 13-1-19 |
| shēngyì | 生意 | 生意 | 12-2-4 |
| shénme | 什麼 | 什么 | 1-2-6 |
| shì | 是 | 是 | 1-1-6 |
| shì | 試 | 试 | 12-2-11 |
| shī | 濕 | 湿 | 14-2-6 |
| shì a | 是啊 | 是啊 | 5-1-18 |
| shí'èryuè dǐ | 十二月底 | 十二月底 | 14-1-18 |
| shìde | 是的 | 是的 | 1-1-21 |
| shíhòu | 時候 | 时候 | 7-1-10 |

| Pinyin | Traditional Characters | Simplified Characters | Lesson-Dialogue-Number |
|---|---|---|---|
| shíjiān | 時間 | 时间 | 12-1-4 |
| shìshìkàn | 試試看 | 试试看 | 12-2-15 |
| shōudào | 收到 | 收到 | 11-2-14 |
| shǒujī | 手機 | 手机 | 4-2-3 |
| shū | 書 | 书 | 2-2-5 |
| shūfǎ | 書法 | 书法 | 7-2-13 |
| shūfú | 舒服 | 舒服 | 8-1-14 |
| shuì | 睡 | 睡 | 15-2-17 |
| shuǐ | 水 | 水 | 15-1-18 |
| shuǐguǒ | 水果 | 水果 | 10-1-1 |
| shuìjiào | 睡覺 | 睡觉 | 15-1-20 |
| shuō | 說 | 说 | 5-1-5 |
| suǒyǐ | 所以 | 所以 | 5-2-6 |
| sùshè | 宿舍 | 宿舍 | 6-2-11 |

**T**

| Pinyin | Traditional Characters | Simplified Characters | Lesson-Dialogue-Number |
|---|---|---|---|
| tā | 他 | 他 | 1-2-10 |
| tā | 她 | 她 | 9-2-5 |
| tài | 太 | 太 | 4-2-4 |
| tài hǎo le | 太好了 | 太好了 | 5-1-21 |
| tài kèqì | 太客氣 | 太客气 | 13-1-23 |
| Táidōng | 臺東 | 台东 | 9-1-14 |
| táifēng | 颱風 | 台风 | 14-2-3 |
| Táinán | 臺南 | 台南 | 8-1-17 |
| tàitai | 太太 | 太太 | 10-2-7 |
| Táiwān | 臺灣（＝台灣） | 台湾（＝台湾） | 1-1-18 |
| tāmen | 他們 | 他们 | 6-1-1 |
| tāng | 湯 | 汤 | 5-1-10 |
| tàofáng | 套房 | 套房 | 11-1-16 |
| tǎoyàn | 討厭 | 讨厌 | 14-2-7 |
| tèbié | 特別 | 特别 | 9-2-11 |
| tì | 替 | 替 | 12-1-14 |
| tī | 踢 | 踢 | 3-1-13 |
| tián | 甜 | 甜 | 10-1-7 |
| tiān | 天 | 天 | 7-2-12 |
| tiándiǎn | 甜點 | 甜点 | 5-2-11 |
| tiānqì | 天氣 | 天气 | 14-1-1 |
| Tiánzhōng Chéngyī | 田中誠一 | 田中诚一 | 2-2-1 |

| Pinyin | Traditional Characters | Simplified Characters | Lesson-Dialogue-Number |
|---|---|---|---|
| tíng | 停 | 停 | 14-2-13 |
| tīng | 聽 | 听 | 3-1-2 |
| tīngshuō | 聽說 | 听说 | 6-1-23 |
| tòng | 痛 | 痛 | 15-1-6 |
| tóngxué | 同學 | 同学 | 8-2-1 |
| tóu | 頭 | 头 | 15-1-5 |
| tù | 吐 | 吐 | 15-2-4 |
| túshūguǎn | 圖書館 | 图书馆 | 6-2-15 |

**W**

| Pinyin | Traditional Characters | Simplified Characters | Lesson-Dialogue-Number |
|---|---|---|---|
| wàidài | 外帶 | 外带 | 4-1-18 |
| wàimiàn | 外面 | 外面 | 6-2-7 |
| wán | 玩 | 玩 | 8-1-4 |
| wàn | 萬 | 万 | 4-2-15 |
| wǎn | 碗 | 碗 | 5-1-17 |
| wǎnfàn | 晚飯 | 晚饭 | 3-2-15 |
| wǎng | 往 | 往 | 10-2-14 |
| Wáng Kāiwén | 王開文 | 王开文 | 1-1-3 |
| wàngle | 忘（了） | 忘（了） | 13-1-6 |
| wǎnglù shàng | 網路上 | 网路上 | 8-1-19 |
| wǎngqiú | 網球 | 网球 | 3-1-6 |
| wǎnshàng | 晚上 | 晚上 | 3-2-3 |
| wànshì rúyì | 萬事如意 | 万事如意 | 13-2-16 |
| wéi | 喂 | 喂 | 11-2-1 |
| wéibō | 微波 | 微波 | 4-1-14 |
| wèikǒu | 胃口 | 胃口 | 15-1-7 |
| wèishénme | 為什麼 | 为什么 | 4-2-17 |
| wèn | 問 | 问 | 7-2-19 |
| wèntí | 問題 | 问题 | 11-2-5 |
| wǒ | 我 | 我 | 1-1-11 |
| wǒ jiù shì | 我就是 | 我就是 | 13-1-20 |
| wǒmen | 我們 | 我们 | 1-1-10 |
| wǔ | 五 | 五 | 2-2-14 |
| wǔcān | 午餐 | 午餐 | 7-2-2 |
| Wūlóng chá | 烏龍茶 | 乌龙茶 | 1-2-15 |

**X**

| Pinyin | Traditional Characters | Simplified Characters | Lesson-Dialogue-Number |
|---|---|---|---|
| xià cì | 下次 | 下次 | 7-1-13 |
| xià ge xīngqí | 下個星期 | 下个星期 | 9-1-11 |
| xiàkè | 下課 | 下课 | 7-2-4 |

| Pinyin | Traditional Characters | Simplified Characters | Lesson-Dialogue-Number |
|---|---|---|---|
| xiān | 先 | 先 | 12-1-5 |
| xiǎng | 想 | 想 | 3-2-7 |
| xiǎng | 想 | 想 | 11-1-18 |
| xiǎng | 想 | 想 | 14-1-6 |
| xiāng | 香 | 香 | 10-1-6 |
| xiānshēng | 先生 | 先生 | 1-1-13 |
| xiànzài | 現在 | 现在 | 6-1-16 |
| xiào | 笑 | 笑 | 10-2-2 |
| xiǎo | 小 | 小 | 4-1-12 |
| xiǎochī | 小吃 | 小吃 | 5-1-8 |
| xiǎojiě | 小姐 | 小姐 | 1-1-7 |
| xiǎolóngbāo | 小籠包 | 小笼包 | 5-1-19 |
| xiǎoshí | 小時 | 小时 | 15-2-18 |
| xiǎoxīn | 小心 | 小心 | 14-2-11 |
| xiàtiān | 夏天 | 夏天 | 14-2-5 |
| xiàwǔ | 下午 | 下午 | 7-2-5 |
| xiàxuě | 下雪 | 下雪 | 14-1-17 |
| xiàyǔ | 下雨 | 下雨 | 14-2-14 |
| Xībānyá | 西班牙 | 西班牙 | 13-1-18 |
| Xībānyá wén | 西班牙文 | 西班牙文 | 13-1-13 |
| xiě | 寫 | 写 | 7-2-17 |
| xièxie | 謝謝 | 谢谢 | 1-1-22 |
| xīguā | 西瓜 | 西瓜 | 10-1-9 |
| xíguàn | 習慣 | 习惯 | 11-2-4 |
| xǐhuān | 喜歡 | 喜欢 | 1-2-8 |
| xīn | 新 | 新 | 4-2-2 |
| xìng | 姓 | 姓 | 1-1-15 |
| xīngqí | 星期 | 星期 | 9-1-1 |
| xīnnián | 新年 | 新年 | 14-1-7 |
| xīnwén | 新聞 | 新闻 | 14-2-8 |
| xīnxiǎng shìchéng | 心想事成 | 心想事成 | 13-2-17 |
| xiōngdì | 兄弟 | 兄弟 | 2-2-12 |
| xiūxí | 休息 | 休息 | 15-1-19 |
| xīwàng | 希望 | 希望 | 12-1-15 |
| xué | 學 | 学 | 3-2-11 |
| xuéfèi | 學費 | 学费 | 12-1-12 |
| xuéshēng | 學生 | 学生 | 6-2-4 |

| Pinyin | Traditional Characters | Simplified Characters | Lesson-Dialogue-Number |
|---|---|---|---|
| xuéxiào | 學校 | 学校 | 6-1-2 |
| xūyào | 需要 | 需要 | 12-1-8 |

## Y

| Pinyin | Traditional Characters | Simplified Characters | Lesson-Dialogue-Number |
|---|---|---|---|
| yào | 要 | 要 | 1-2-13 |
| yào | 要 | 要 | 4-1-9 |
| yào | 要 | 要 | 4-2-14 |
| yào | 要 | 要 | 14-2-4 |
| yào | 藥 | 药 | 15-1-14 |
| yàojú | 藥局 | 药局 | 15-1-15 |
| yàoshì | 要是 | 要是 | 9-2-14 |
| yě | 也 | 也 | 3-1-12 |
| yèshì | 夜市 | 夜市 | 9-2-8 |
| yìdiǎn | 一點 | 一点 | 13-2-8 |
| yídìng | 一定 | 一定 | 5-1-15 |
| yīfú | 衣服 | 衣服 | 10-2-5 |
| yígòng | 一共 | 一共 | 4-1-1 |
| yǐhòu | 以後 | 以后 | 12-1-16 |
| yǐhòu | 以後 | 以后 | 12-2-5 |
| yǐjīng | 已經 | 已经 | 11-2-3 |
| yīnggāi | 應該 | 应该 | 9-2-9 |
| yǐngpiàn | 影片 | 影片 | 9-1-5 |
| yínháng | 銀行 | 银行 | 7-1-9 |
| yīnwèi | 因為 | 因为 | 10-2-16 |
| yīnyuè | 音樂 | 音乐 | 3-1-3 |
| yìqǐ | 一起 | 一起 | 3-2-13 |
| yǐqián | 以前 | 以前 | 10-1-12 |
| yīshēng | 醫生 | 医生 | 15-1-1 |
| yíyàng | 一樣 | 一样 | 13-1-14 |
| yìzhí | 一直 | 一直 | 15-1-2 |
| yóu | 油 | 油 | 15-2-12 |
| yòu | 又 | 又 | 8-1-13 |
| yǒu | 有 | 有 | 2-1-10 |
| yǒu kòng | 有空 | 有空 | 7-1-16 |
| yǒu shì | 有事 | 有事 | 7-2-21 |
| yǒu shíhòu | 有時候 | 有时候 | 9-1-12 |
| yǒu yìdiǎn | 有一點 | 有一点 | 5-2-16 |
| yǒu yìsi | 有意思 | 有意思 | 7-2-22 |

| Pinyin | Traditional Characters | Simplified Characters | Lesson-Dialogue-Number |
|---|---|---|---|
| yòubiān | 右邊 | 右边 | 11-1-6 |
| yǒumíng | 有名 | 有名 | 5-1-7 |
| yǒuxiàn diànshì | 有線電視 | 有线电视 | 11-2-17 |
| yóuyǒng | 游泳 | 游泳 | 3-1-9 |
| yóuyǒngchí | 游泳池 | 游泳池 | 6-2-18 |
| yǔ | 雨 | 雨 | 14-2-1 |
| yuǎn | 遠 | 远 | 6-1-6 |
| yuè | 月 | 月 | 9-2-2 |
| Yuènán | 越南 | 越南 | 3-2-17 |
| yùndòng | 運動 | 运动 | 3-1-4 |
| Yùshān | 玉山 | 玉山 | 14-1-15 |
| yùshì | 浴室 | 浴室 | 11-1-7 |
| yǔyán | 語言 | 语言 | 13-1-9 |
| yǔyán zhōngxīn | 語言中心 | 语言中心 | 12-1-21 |

### Z

| Pinyin | Traditional Characters | Simplified Characters | Lesson-Dialogue-Number |
|---|---|---|---|
| zài | 在 | 在 | 6-1-3 |
| zài | 在 | 在 | 6-2-5 |
| zài | 在 | 在 | 7-2-1 |
| zài | 載 | 载 | 8-2-6 |
| zài | 再 | 再 | 11-1-19 |
| zài | 再 | 再 | 12-2-14 |
| zàijiàn | 再見 | 再见 | 7-1-17 |
| zǎo yìdiǎn | 早一點 | 早一点 | 15-1-21 |
| zǎoshàng | 早上 | 早上 | 3-1-18 |
| zěnme | 怎麼 | 怎么 | 8-1-5 |
| zěnme | 怎麼 | 怎么 | 13-1-5 |
| zěnme le | 怎麼了 | 怎么了 | 15-2-19 |
| zěnmeyàng | 怎麼樣 | 怎么样 | 3-1-20 |
| zhàn | 站 | 站 | 8-1-15 |
| zhāng | 張 | 张 | 2-1-15 |
| Zhāng Yíjūn | 張怡君 | 张怡君 | 2-1-1 |
| zhǎo | 找 | 找 | 6-1-19 |
| zhǎo | 找 | 找 | 12-2-7 |
| zhàopiàn | 照片 | 照片 | 2-1-12 |
| zhàoxiàng | 照相 | 照相 | 2-1-14 |
| zhè / zhèi | 這 | 这 | 1-1-12 |
| zhè cì | 這次 | 这次 | 14-2-15 |
| zhèlǐ | 這裡 | 这里 | 6-2-3 |
| zhème | 這麼 | 这么 | 5-1-11 |

| Pinyin | Traditional Characters | Simplified Characters | Lesson-Dialogue-Number |
|---|---|---|---|
| zhēn | 真 | 真 | 5-1-3 |
| zhēnde | 真的 | 真的 | 6-1-14 |
| zhèxiē | 這些 | 这些 | 10-2-19 |
| zhèyàng | 這樣 | 这样 | 12-2-9 |
| zhǐ | 只 | 只 | 14-1-14 |
| zhī | 支 | 支 | 4-2-1 |
| zhīdào | 知道 | 知道 | 5-1-12 |
| zhǒng | 種 | 种 | 4-2-7 |
| zhōng | 中 | 中 | 4-1-11 |
| Zhōngguó | 中國 | 中国 | 8-2-10 |
| zhōngtóu | 鐘頭 | 钟头 | 8-1-7 |
| Zhōngwén | 中文 | 中文 | 3-2-12 |
| zhōngwǔ | 中午 | 中午 | 7-1-7 |
| zhōumò | 週末 | 周末 | 3-1-1 |
| zhù | 住 | 住 | 10-2-17 |
| zhù | 祝 | 祝 | 13-2-13 |
| zhuāng | 裝 | 装 | 11-2-11 |
| zhūjiǎo | 豬腳 | 猪脚 | 13-2-5 |
| zì | 字 | 字 | 7-2-16 |
| zìjǐ | 自己 | 自己 | 5-2-7 |
| zǒulù | 走路 | 走路 | 11-1-9 |
| zū | 租 | 租 | 11-1-1 |
| zuì | 最 | 最 | 5-1-9 |
| zuìhǎo | 最好 | 最好 | 15-2-23 |
| zuìjìn | 最近 | 最近 | 7-2-9 |
| zuò | 坐 | 坐 | 2-1-8 |
| zuò | 坐 | 坐 | 8-1-1 |
| zuò | 做 | 做 | 12-2-3 |
| zuò shénme | 做什麼 | 做什么 | 3-1-22 |
| zuǒbiān | 左邊 | 左边 | 11-1-5 |
| zuòfàn | 做飯 | 做饭 | 5-2-8 |
| zuótiān | 昨天 | 昨天 | 5-2-1 |
| zuǒyòu | 左右 | 左右 | 13-1-16 |
| zúqiú | 足球 | 足球 | 3-1-14 |

| English definition | Traditional Characters | Simplified Characters | Lesson-Dialogue-Number |
|---|---|---|---|
| **A** | | | |
| a bit earlier | 早一點 | 早一点 | 15-1-21 |
| (a) few | 幾 | 几 | 15-2-5 |
| a little | 有一點 | 有一点 | 5-2-16 |
| a little, some | 一點 | 一点 | 13-2-8 |
| about the same | 差不多 | 差不多 | 8-2-14 |
| to access the internet, to use the internet | 上網 | 上网 | 4-2-9 |
| afternoon | 下午 | 下午 | 7-2-5 |
| afterwards | 以後 | 以后 | 12-2-5 |
| again | 再 | 再 | 12-2-14 |
| all, both | 都 | 都 | 2-1-13 |
| already | 已經 | 已经 | 11-2-3 |
| also | 也 | 也 | 3-1-12 |
| altogether | 一共 | 一共 | 4-1-1 |
| America | 美國 | 美国 | 1-2-17 |
| ancient times | 古代 | 古代 | 8-2-3 |
| and, as well as | 和 | 和 | 3-1-8 |
| annoying | 討厭 | 讨厌 | 14-2-7 |
| appetite | 胃口 | 胃口 | 15-1-7 |
| approximately | 左右 | 左右 | 13-1-16 |
| approximately, about, probably | 大概 | 大概 | 9-1-9 |
| arrive | 到 | 到 | 11-1-12 |
| to ask | 問 | 问 | 7-2-19 |
| at | 在 | 在 | 6-2-5 |
| aunt; here a polite term for a friend's mother regardless of age | 伯母 | 伯母 | 2-2-2 |
| autumn (season) | 秋天 | 秋天 | 14-1-12 |
| **B** | | | |
| back | 後面 | 后面 | 6-1-12 |
| bank | 銀行 | 银行 | 7-1-9 |
| baseball | 棒球 | 棒球 | 3-1-7 |
| basketball | 籃球 | 篮球 | 3-1-11 |

| English definition | Traditional Characters | Simplified Characters | Lesson-Dialogue-Number |
|---|---|---|---|
| bathroom | 浴室 | 浴室 | 11-1-7 |
| to be | 是 | 是 | 1-1-6 |
| to be able to, can | 會 | 会 | 5-2-10 |
| beautiful | 美 | 美 | 6-1-9 |
| because | 因為 | 因为 | 10-2-16 |
| beef | 牛肉 | 牛肉 | 5-1-1 |
| before | 以前 | 以前 | 10-1-12 |
| to begin, to start | 開始 | 开始 | 7-2-15 |
| birthday | 生日 | 生日 | 13-1-1 |
| blue | 藍色 | 蓝色 | 10-2-15 |
| book | 書 | 书 | 2-2-5 |
| both...and... | 又 | 又 | 8-1-13 |
| a bowl of | 碗 | 碗 | 5-1-17 |
| boy-, male- | 男 | 男 | 10-2-8 |
| brothers | 兄弟 | 兄弟 | 2-2-12 |
| bus | 公共汽車（公車） | 公共汽车（公车） | 8-2-11 |
| business | 生意 | 生意 | 12-2-4 |
| busy | 忙 | 忙 | 7-2-10 |
| to be busy, to be engaged | 有事 | 有事 | 7-2-21 |
| but, however | 可是 | 可是 | 5-2-3 |
| but, however | 但是 | 但是 | 8-1-12 |
| to buy | 買 | 买 | 4-1-5 |
| by the way | 對了 | 对了 | 7-1-15 |
| Bye. Take care. | 慢走 | 慢走 | 14-2-17 |
| **C** | | | |
| cable TV | 有線電視 | 有线电视 | 11-2-17 |
| cake | 蛋糕 | 蛋糕 | 13-2-11 |
| to be called, i.e., to have the first name xx | 叫 | 叫 | 1-1-16 |
| calligraphy | 書法 | 书法 | 7-2-13 |
| can, to be able to | 能 | 能 | 4-2-8 |
| to be careful, to take care | 小心 | 小心 | 14-2-11 |
| to catch/have a cold | 感冒 | 感冒 | 15-1-13 |

| English definition | Traditional Characters | Simplified Characters | Lesson-Dialogue-Number |
|---|---|---|---|
| to celebrate | 過 | 过 | 13-1-15 |
| cell phone | 手機 | 手机 | 4-2-3 |
| certainly, of course | 當然 | 当然 | 13-1-8 |
| character | 字 | 字 | 7-2-16 |
| cheap, inexpensive | 便宜 | 便宜 | 4-2-13 |
| China | 中國 | 中国 | 8-2-10 |
| Chinese language | 中文 | 中文 | 3-2-12 |
| Chinese last name, common in Taiwan | 林 | 林 | 11-1-22 |
| class | 課 | 课 | 7-2-14 |
| classmate | 同學 | 同学 | 8-2-1 |
| classroom | 教室 | 教室 | 6-2-17 |
| clean | 乾淨 | 干净 | 10-2-12 |
| clothes | 衣服 | 衣服 | 10-2-5 |
| coffee | 咖啡 | 咖啡 | 1-2-14 |
| cold | 風 | 风 | 14-1-2 |
| to come | 來 | 来 | 1-1-5 |
| to come back | 回來 | 回来 | 13-1-3 |
| comfortable | 舒服 | 舒服 | 8-1-14 |
| company | 公司 | 公司 | 12-1-13 |
| complement marker | 得 | 得 | 5-2-9 |
| to be concerned about | 關心 | 关心 | 15-2-15 |
| continuously, all the way | 一直 | 一直 | 15-1-2 |
| convenience store | 便利商店 | 便利商店 | 8-1-20 |
| convenient | 方便 | 方便 | 6-2-2 |
| to cook | 做飯 | 做饭 | 5-2-8 |
| correct, right | 對 | 对 | 10-1-11 |
| could (possibility) | 可以 | 可以 | 3-2-10 |
| could (possibility) | 可以 | 可以 | 5-2-13 |
| country | 國家 | 国家 | 12-2-10 |
| cuisine | 菜 | 菜 | 3-2-16 |
| cup | 杯 | 杯 | 4-1-6 |

**D**

| English definition | Traditional Characters | Simplified Characters | Lesson-Dialogue-Number |
|---|---|---|---|
| Da-an (name of a KTV named after a district in Taipei, where Shida is also located) | 大安 | 大安 | 7-1-12 |
| dad | 爸爸 | 爸爸 | 2-1-20 |

| English definition | Traditional Characters | Simplified Characters | Lesson-Dialogue-Number |
|---|---|---|---|
| date, day of a month | 號 | 号 | 9-2-3 |
| to decide | 決定 | 决定 | 9-2-13 |
| delicious | 好吃 | 好吃 | 5-1-4 |
| dessert | 甜點 | 甜点 | 5-2-11 |
| dinner | 晚飯 | 晚饭 | 3-2-15 |
| disposal marker | 把 | 把 | 15-1-17 |
| do what | 做什麼 | 做什么 | 3-1-22 |
| to do, to engage in | 做 | 做 | 12-2-3 |
| doctor | 醫生 | 医生 | 15-1-1 |
| Don't mention it. It's my pleasure. | 哪裡，哪裡 | 哪里，哪里 | 13-2-14 |
| don't (used in imperatives) | 別 | 别 | 15-2-14 |
| dormitory | 宿舍 | 宿舍 | 6-2-11 |
| downstairs | 樓下 | 楼下 | 6-1-18 |
| to drink | 喝 | 喝 | 1-2-2 |

**E**

| English definition | Traditional Characters | Simplified Characters | Lesson-Dialogue-Number |
|---|---|---|---|
| easy to | 好 | 好 | 12-2-6 |
| to eat | 吃 | 吃 | 3-2-14 |
| egg | 蛋 | 蛋 | 13-2-7 |
| the end of December | 十二月底 | 十二月底 | 14-1-18 |
| with enthusiasm | 熱心 | 热心 | 13-1-12 |
| even (more, less, etc.) | 更 | 更 | 14-2-9 |
| evening, night | 晚上 | 晚上 | 3-2-3 |
| every, each | 每 | 每 | 7-2-11 |
| everyone | 大家 | 大家 | 14-2-10 |
| Excellent. Great. | 太好了 | 太好了 | 5-1-21 |
| to exchange | 交換 | 交换 | 13-1-10 |
| to exercise | 運動 | 运动 | 3-1-4 |
| expensive | 貴 | 贵 | 4-2-11 |
| extra fine noodles | 麵線 | 面线 | 13-2-6 |

**F**

| English definition | Traditional Characters | Simplified Characters | Lesson-Dialogue-Number |
|---|---|---|---|
| to fall ill | 生病 | 生病 | 15-1-11 |
| family (members) | 家人 | 家人 | 2-1-4 |
| far | 遠 | 远 | 6-1-6 |
| fast | 快 | 快 | 8-1-9 |
| to feel, to think | 覺得 | 觉得 | 3-1-15 |
| few in number | 少 | 少 | 5-1-6 |
| film | 影片 | 影片 | 9-1-5 |

| English definition | Traditional Characters | Simplified Characters | Lesson-Dialogue-Number |
|---|---|---|---|
| fine, well | 好 | 好 | 1-1-14 |
| to finish | 結束 | 结束 | 7-2-8 |
| to finish class | 下課 | 下课 | 7-2-4 |
| first | 先 | 先 | 12-1-5 |
| five | 五 | 五 | 2-2-14 |
| to flow | 流 | 流 | 15-1-3 |
| for | 幫 | 帮 | 4-1-13 |
| for here | 內用 | 內用 | 4-1-19 |
| for, on behalf of | 替 | 替 | 12-1-14 |
| to forget | 忘（了） | 忘（了） | 13-1-6 |
| fragrant | 香 | 香 | 10-1-6 |
| friend | 朋友 | 朋友 | 6-1-20 |
| from | 從 | 从 | 7-1-6 |
| front | 前面 | 前面 | 6-1-10 |
| fruit | 水果 | 水果 | 10-1-1 |
| in the future | 以後 | 以后 | 12-1-16 |

**G**

| English definition | Traditional Characters | Simplified Characters | Lesson-Dialogue-Number |
|---|---|---|---|
| game, competition | 比賽 | 比赛 | 7-2-7 |
| gate, entrance | 門口 | 门口 | 13-1-17 |
| general measure word | 個 | 个 | 2-2-10 |
| to get | 拿 | 拿 | 15-1-16 |
| to get settled down, to get used to | 習慣 | 习惯 | 11-2-4 |
| gift, present | 禮物 | 礼物 | 13-2-1 |
| girl-, female- | 女 | 女 | 9-2-1 |
| to give | 給 | 给 | 10-1-4 |
| to give someone a ride to someone on / in a vehicle e.g. bicycle or car | 載 | 载 | 8-2-6 |
| to give it a try, to try and see what happens | 試試看 | 试试看 | 12-2-15 |
| to go | 去 | 去 | 3-1-19 |
| to go back, to return | 回去 | 回去 | 11-1-17 |
| go home | 回家 | 回家 | 15-2-22 |
| to go out | 出去 | 出去 | 9-1-8 |
| to go to class | 上課 | 上课 | 6-1-21 |
| to go to work | 上班 | 上班 | 12-1-18 |
| to go/come to | 到 | 到 | 12-1-17 |

| English definition | Traditional Characters | Simplified Characters | Lesson-Dialogue-Number |
|---|---|---|---|
| to go/stay with somebody, to accompany | 陪 | 陪 | 15-2-7 |
| Goodbye. | 再見 | 再见 | 7-1-17 |
| good-looking | 好看 | 好看 | 2-1-16 |
| grades | 成績 | 成绩 | 12-1-11 |

**H**

| English definition | Traditional Characters | Simplified Characters | Lesson-Dialogue-Number |
|---|---|---|---|
| half | 半 | 半 | 7-2-6 |
| happy | 開心 | 开心 | 10-2-3 |
| happy | 快樂 | 快乐 | 13-1-2 |
| Happy Birthday. | 生日快樂 | 生日快乐 | 13-1-19 |
| hard to, difficult to | 難 | 难 | 12-2-12 |
| to have | 有 | 有 | 2-1-10 |
| to have a fever | 發燒 | 发烧 | 15-1-12 |
| to have a holiday | 放假 | 放假 | 9-1-10 |
| to have a meal | 吃飯 | 吃饭 | 6-2-10 |
| to have a taste, try it, taste it | 吃吃看 | 吃吃看 | 10-1-15 |
| to have free time | 有空 | 有空 | 7-1-16 |
| to have fun | 玩 | 玩 | 8-1-4 |
| to have to, must | 得 | 得 | 7-1-8 |
| he, him | 他 | 他 | 1-2-10 |
| head | 頭 | 头 | 15-1-5 |
| health | 健康 | 健康 | 15-2-9 |
| health center | 健康中心 | 健康中心 | 15-2-21 |
| hear that | 聽說 | 听说 | 6-1-23 |
| here, this place | 這裡 | 这里 | 6-2-3 |
| High Speed Rail (HSR) | 高鐵 | 高铁 | 8-1-18 |
| home, house | 家 | 家 | 2-1-5 |
| homework | 功課 | 功课 | 9-1-7 |
| to hope | 希望 | 希望 | 12-1-15 |
| hot | 熱 | 热 | 4-1-7 |
| hot (spicy) | 辣 | 辣 | 5-2-4 |
| hotel | 旅館 | 旅馆 | 10-2-6 |
| hour | 鐘頭 | 钟头 | 8-1-7 |
| hour | 小時 | 小时 | 15-2-18 |
| house | 房子 | 房子 | 2-1-7 |
| how | 怎麼 | 怎么 | 8-1-5 |

| English definition | Traditional Characters | Simplified Characters | Lesson-Dialogue-Number |
|---|---|---|---|
| How about it? How does that sound? What do you think? | 怎麼樣 | 怎么样 | 3-1-20 |
| How about...? How does that sound? | 好不好 | 好不好 | 3-2-18 |
| How are you? Hello. | 你好 | 你好 | 1-1-23 |
| How come? | 怎麼 | 怎么 | 13-1-5 |
| how long | 多久 | 多久 | 9-1-13 |
| how many | 幾 | 几 | 2-2-9 |
| how much, how many | 多少 | 多少 | 4-1-2 |
| however, but | 不過 | 不过 | 11-2-12 |
| Hualien, name of a city on the eastern coast of Taiwan | 花蓮 | 花莲 | 6-1-22 |
| hundred | 百 | 百 | 4-1-15 |

**I**

| English definition | Traditional Characters | Simplified Characters | Lesson-Dialogue-Number |
|---|---|---|---|
| I, me | 我 | 我 | 1-1-11 |
| I'm sorry. | 對不起 | 对不起 | 1-2-18 |
| icy | 冰 | 冰 | 15-2-13 |
| if | 要是 | 要是 | 9-2-14 |
| to be inflamed | 發炎 | 发炎 | 15-1-10 |
| inside | 裡面 | 里面 | 6-2-8 |
| to install | 裝 | 装 | 11-2-11 |
| insurance | 保險 | 保险 | 15-2-10 |
| interesting, fun | 好玩 | 好玩 | 3-1-16 |
| to be interesting, to be fun | 有意思 | 有意思 | 7-2-22 |
| on the Internet | 網路上 | 网络上 | 8-1-19 |
| It would be best.../ (You) should··· | 最好 | 最好 | 15-2-23 |
| It's not necessary. | 不用了 | 不用了 | 15-2-20 |

**J**

| English definition | Traditional Characters | Simplified Characters | Lesson-Dialogue-Number |
|---|---|---|---|
| Japan | 日本 | 日本 | 1-2-16 |
| job, work | 工作 | 工作 | 12-2-8 |
| just now | 剛 | 刚 | 7-2-3 |

**K**

| English definition | Traditional Characters | Simplified Characters | Lesson-Dialogue-Number |
|---|---|---|---|
| Karaoke | KTV | KTV | 7-1-2 |
| keep up the good work | 加油 | 加油 | 12-1-22 |
| to kick | 踢 | 踢 | 3-1-13 |

| English definition | Traditional Characters | Simplified Characters | Lesson-Dialogue-Number |
|---|---|---|---|
| kind, type | 種 | 种 | 4-2-7 |
| kitchen | 廚房 | 厨房 | 11-1-4 |
| to know | 知道 | 知道 | 5-1-12 |

**L**

| English definition | Traditional Characters | Simplified Characters | Lesson-Dialogue-Number |
|---|---|---|---|
| landlord | 房東 | 房东 | 11-1-2 |
| language | 語言 | 语言 | 13-1-9 |
| language center | 語言中心 | 语言中心 | 12-1-21 |
| large | 大 | 大 | 4-1-10 |
| last month | 上個月 | 上个月 | 10-2-18 |
| last time | 上次 | 上次 | 14-2-16 |
| last year | 去年 | 去年 | 12-2-2 |
| later | 等一下 | 等一下 | 7-2-20 |
| to laugh, to smile | 笑 | 笑 | 10-2-2 |
| to learn, to study | 學 | 学 | 3-2-11 |
| left (side) | 左邊 | 左边 | 11-1-5 |
| library | 圖書館 | 图书馆 | 6-2-15 |
| light repast, snack | 小吃 | 小吃 | 5-1-8 |
| to like | 喜歡 | 喜欢 | 1-2-8 |
| to listen | 聽 | 听 | 3-1-2 |
| living room | 客廳 | 客厅 | 11-1-3 |
| to be located at | 在 | 在 | 6-1-3 |
| long (time) | 久 | 久 | 12-1-3 |
| long time no see | 好久不見 | 好久不见 | 13-1-21 |
| to look for | 找 | 找 | 12-2-7 |
| lunch | 午餐 | 午餐 | 7-2-2 |

**M**

| English definition | Traditional Characters | Simplified Characters | Lesson-Dialogue-Number |
|---|---|---|---|
| to make a phone call | 打電話 | 打电话 | 11-1-23 |
| a man from Japan | 田中誠一 | 田中诚一 | 2-2-1 |
| a man from Taiwan | 李明華 | 李明华 | 1-1-2 |
| a man from the Republic of Honduras | 馬安同 | 马安同 | 2-1-2 |
| a man from the US | 王開文 | 王开文 | 1-1-3 |
| mango | 芒果 | 芒果 | 10-1-3 |
| many | 多 | 多 | 2-1-11 |
| Maokong, name of a must-see place in Taipei to visit for fine tea and scenery | 貓空 | 猫空 | 9-2-16 |
| Mass Rapid Transit (MRT) | 捷運 | 捷运 | 8-2-7 |

| English definition | Traditional Characters | Simplified Characters | Lesson-Dialogue-Number |
|---|---|---|---|
| may (permission) | 可以 | 可以 | 7-2-18 |
| May all your wishes come true. | 心想事成 | 心想事成 | 13-2-17 |
| May everything go your way. | 萬事如意 | 万事如意 | 13-2-16 |
| May I ask you..., Excuse me,… | 請問 | 请问 | 1-1-20 |
| measure word for bags, packages etc. | 包 | 包 | 15-2-16 |
| measure word for cell phones | 支 | 支 | 4-2-1 |
| measure word for Chinese money | 塊 | 块 | 4-1-16 |
| measure word for day | 天 | 天 | 7-2-12 |
| measure word for flat objects (e.g., paper, tickets) | 張 | 张 | 2-1-15 |
| measure word for houses, rooms, etc. | 間 | 间 | 11-1-13 |
| measure word for minutes | 分鐘 | 分钟 | 11-1-10 |
| measure word for pieces of food (e.g., meat, cake) | 塊 | 块 | 10-1-5 |
| measure word for times, occurrences | 次 | 次 | 15-2-6 |
| measure word for year | 年 | 年 | 12-1-2 |
| measure word for buildings | 棟 | 栋 | 6-2-13 |
| measure word for restaurants, shops, etc. | 家 | 家 | 5-1-13 |
| medicine | 藥 | 药 | 15-1-14 |
| medium | 中 | 中 | 4-1-11 |
| to meet | 見面 | 见面 | 7-1-5 |
| to meet, to see | 找 | 找 | 6-1-19 |
| to microwave | 微波 | 微波 | 4-1-14 |
| minute | 分 | 分 | 7-1-4 |
| to miss (someone) | 想 | 想 | 14-1-6 |
| Miss, Ms. | 小姐 | 小姐 | 1-1-7 |
| modification marker | 的 | 的 | 2-1-3 |
| mom | 媽媽 | 妈妈 | 2-1-21 |
| money | 錢 | 钱 | 4-1-3 |

| English definition | Traditional Characters | Simplified Characters | Lesson-Dialogue-Number |
|---|---|---|---|
| month of a year | 月 | 月 | 9-2-2 |
| (comparatively) more | 比較 | 比较 | 8-1-8 |
| morning | 早上 | 早上 | 3-1-18 |
| most | 最 | 最 | 5-1-9 |
| most (of), mostly | 大部分 | 大部分 | 13-2-15 |
| motorcycle, scooter | 機車 | 机车 | 8-2-5 |
| mountain | 山 | 山 | 6-1-13 |
| on a mountain, in the mountains | 山上 | 山上 | 6-1-4 |
| movie | 電影 | 电影 | 3-2-5 |
| Mr. | 先生 | 先生 | 1-1-13 |
| a multi-storey building | 大樓 | 大楼 | 6-2-14 |
| music | 音樂 | 音乐 | 3-1-3 |

**N**

| English definition | Traditional Characters | Simplified Characters | Lesson-Dialogue-Number |
|---|---|---|---|
| name | 名字 | 名字 | 2-2-4 |
| National Palace Museum | 故宮博物院（故宮） | 故宫博物院（故宫） | 8-2-9 |
| near | 近 | 近 | 6-2-1 |
| to need | 需要 | 需要 | 12-1-8 |
| new | 新 | 新 | 4-2-2 |
| New Year | 新年 | 新年 | 14-1-7 |
| New York | 紐約 | 纽约 | 14-1-16 |
| news | 新聞 | 新闻 | 14-2-8 |
| next time | 下次 | 下次 | 7-1-13 |
| next week | 下個星期 | 下个星期 | 9-1-11 |
| next year | 明年 | 明年 | 14-1-11 |
| night market | 夜市 | 夜市 | 9-2-8 |
| No need to stand on formalities, i.e., It's my pleasure. | 不必客氣 | 不必客气 | 13-1-22 |
| No problem. | 沒問題 | 没问题 | 7-1-14 |
| noodles | 麵 | 面 | 5-1-2 |
| noon | 中午 | 中午 | 7-1-7 |
| not | 不 | 不 | 1-2-11 |
| not | 沒 | 没 | 2-2-11 |
| Not a problem. | 沒關係 | 没关系 | 11-2-16 |
| not bad | 不錯 | 不错 | 5-2-12 |
| (here) to not like, to fear | 怕 | 怕 | 5-2-5 |

| English definition | Traditional Characters | Simplified Characters | Lesson-Dialogue-Number |
|---|---|---|---|
| not to look good | 難看 | 难看 | 15-2-2 |
| not well | 不好 | 不好 | 5-2-17 |
| now | 現在 | 现在 | 6-1-16 |

### O

| English definition | Traditional Characters | Simplified Characters | Lesson-Dialogue-Number |
|---|---|---|---|
| O.K. | 好啊 | 好啊 | 3-1-23 |
| O.K. | 好的 | 好的 | 4-1-17 |
| O.K. | 好 | 好 | 2-1-9 |
| ocean | 海 | 海 | 6-1-11 |
| o'clock | 點 | 点 | 7-1-1 |
| often | 常 | 常 | 3-1-10 |
| oily, greasy | 油 | 油 | 15-2-12 |
| old | 舊 | 旧 | 4-2-5 |
| older brother | 哥哥 | 哥哥 | 2-2-6 |
| older sister | 姐姐 | 姐姐 | 2-1-18 |
| only, merely | 就 | 就 | 11-1-11 |
| only, merely | 只 | 只 | 14-1-14 |
| Oolong tea | 烏龍茶 | 乌龙茶 | 1-2-15 |
| opportunity | 機會 | 机会 | 10-1-13 |
| or | 或是 | 或是 | 8-1-16 |
| or (used in a question) | 還是 | 还是 | 3-2-8 |
| to order (meals) | 點 | 点 | 5-1-16 |
| to order (something in advance) | 訂 | 订 | 13-2-3 |
| outside | 外面 | 外面 | 6-2-7 |

### P

| English definition | Traditional Characters | Simplified Characters | Lesson-Dialogue-Number |
|---|---|---|---|
| painful | 痛 | 痛 | 15-1-6 |
| parents | 父母 | 父母 | 14-1-9 |
| a particle indicating a realization | 啊 | 啊 | 13-1-4 |
| a particle used in addressing people, especially over the phone | 喂 | 喂 | 11-2-1 |
| to pay | 付 | 付 | 11-2-13 |
| person, people | 人 | 人 | 1-2-7 |
| a person's "color" (said of the face when healthy or sick, pleased or angry etc.) | 臉色 | 脸色 | 15-2-1 |
| pharmacy, drug store | 藥局 | 药局 | 15-1-15 |
| photo | 照片 | 照片 | 2-1-12 |

| English definition | Traditional Characters | Simplified Characters | Lesson-Dialogue-Number |
|---|---|---|---|
| to pick sb up | 接 | 接 | 1-1-9 |
| place | 地方 | 地方 | 6-1-15 |
| to plan to | 打算 | 打算 | 9-1-3 |
| to plan to | 計畫 | 计划 | 12-1-1 |
| to play (ball games) | 打 | 打 | 3-1-5 |
| please | 請 | 请 | 1-2-1 |
| Please come in! | 請進 | 请进 | 2-1-22 |
| poor, bad | 差 | 差 | 15-1-8 |
| pork knuckles | 豬腳 | 猪脚 | 13-2-5 |
| pretty | 漂亮 | 漂亮 | 2-1-6 |
| problem, question | 問題 | 问题 | 11-2-5 |
| progressive aspect verb; in the process of doing something | 在 | 在 | 7-2-1 |

### R

| English definition | Traditional Characters | Simplified Characters | Lesson-Dialogue-Number |
|---|---|---|---|
| rain | 雨 | 雨 | 14-2-1 |
| to rain | 下雨 | 下雨 | 14-2-14 |
| to read | 看書 | 看书 | 2-2-8 |
| really | 真 | 真 | 5-1-3 |
| really must, definitely | 一定 | 一定 | 5-1-15 |
| really, truly | 真的 | 真的 | 6-1-14 |
| to receive | 收到 | 收到 | 11-2-14 |
| recently, lately | 最近 | 最近 | 7-2-9 |
| red | 紅色 | 红色 | 10-1-8 |
| red maple leaves | 紅葉 | 红叶 | 14-1-13 |
| to remember | 記得 | 记得 | 13-1-7 |
| to rent | 租 | 租 | 11-1-1 |
| rent (for a room or a house) | 房租 | 房租 | 11-2-2 |
| restaurant | 餐廳 | 餐厅 | 5-2-2 |
| to return to one's country | 回國 | 回国 | 9-1-2 |
| to ride | 騎 | 骑 | 8-2-4 |
| right (side) | 右邊 | 右边 | 11-1-6 |
| room | 房間 | 房间 | 11-1-15 |

### S

| English definition | Traditional Characters | Simplified Characters | Lesson-Dialogue-Number |
|---|---|---|---|
| say | 說 | 说 | 5-1-5 |
| scary | 可怕 | 可怕 | 14-2-12 |
| scenery, landscape | 風景 | 风景 | 6-1-8 |
| scholarship | 獎學金 | 奖学金 | 12-1-10 |

| English definition | Traditional Characters | Simplified Characters | Lesson-Dialogue-Number |
|---|---|---|---|
| school | 學校 | 学校 | 6-1-2 |
| to see a doctor | 看病 | 看病 | 15-2-8 |
| to see, to watch | 看 | 看 | 3-2-4 |
| to seem to be, to appear to be (often used to take the edge off of a comment) | 好像 | 好像 | 11-2-7 |
| self | 自己 | 自己 | 5-2-7 |
| to sell | 賣 | 卖 | 4-2-12 |
| sentence final particle | 嗎 | 吗 | 1-1-8 |
| sentence final particle | 呢 | 呢 | 1-2-9 |
| sentence-final particle | 啊 | 啊 | 3-1-21 |
| sentence-final particle for guessing | 吧 | 吧 | 10-1-10 |
| sentence-final particle for suggestion | 吧 | 吧 | 3-2-9 |
| sentence-final particle indicating the speaker's sense of certainty | 了 | 了 | 4-2-6 |
| she, her | 她 | 她 | 9-2-5 |
| shop, store | 店 | 店 | 5-1-14 |
| short (height) | 矮 | 矮 | 10-2-9 |
| should | 應該 | 应该 | 9-2-9 |
| (by the) side, next to | 旁邊 | 旁边 | 6-2-16 |
| to sing | 唱歌 | 唱歌 | 7-1-3 |
| sisters | 姐妹 | 姐妹 | 2-2-13 |
| to sit | 坐 | 坐 | 2-1-8 |
| to ski | 滑雪 | 滑雪 | 14-1-4 |
| to sleep | 睡覺 | 睡觉 | 15-1-20 |
| to sleep | 睡 | 睡 | 15-2-17 |
| slow | 慢 | 慢 | 8-1-6 |
| small | 小 | 小 | 4-1-12 |
| snot, nasal mucus, a running nose | 鼻水 | 鼻水 | 15-1-4 |
| to snow | 下雪 | 下雪 | 14-1-17 |
| so | 這麼 | 这么 | 5-1-11 |
| so (very) | 那麼 | 那么 | 13-1-11 |
| soccer | 足球 | 足球 | 3-1-14 |
| sometimes | 有時候 | 有时候 | 9-1-12 |
| soon | 快 | 快 | 14-1-8 |
| sorry | 不好意思 | 不好意思 | 11-2-15 |

| English definition | Traditional Characters | Simplified Characters | Lesson-Dialogue-Number |
|---|---|---|---|
| soup, broth | 湯 | 汤 | 5-1-10 |
| Spain | 西班牙 | 西班牙 | 13-1-18 |
| the Spanish language | 西班牙文 | 西班牙文 | 13-1-13 |
| special | 特別 | 特别 | 9-2-11 |
| to spend (time or money) | 花 | 花 | 12-1-9 |
| spring (season) | 春天 | 春天 | 14-1-5 |
| station | 站 | 站 | 8-1-15 |
| to stay | 住 | 住 | 10-2-17 |
| steamed buns with meat stuffing filling | 包子 | 包子 | 4-1-8 |
| still, additionally | 還 | 还 | 9-2-6 |
| stinky tofu (fermented tofu) | 臭豆腐 | 臭豆腐 | 5-1-20 |
| stomach, abdomen | 肚子 | 肚子 | 15-2-3 |
| to stop | 停 | 停 | 14-2-13 |
| store, shop | 商店 | 商店 | 6-2-9 |
| store-owner, boss | 老闆 | 老板 | 4-1-4 |
| a storey, a floor | 樓 | 楼 | 6-2-12 |
| student | 學生 | 学生 | 6-2-4 |
| to study | 念 | 念 | 12-1-6 |
| to study | 念書 | 念书 | 12-1-19 |
| suggestion | 建議 | 建议 | 9-2-7 |
| suite, studio | 套房 | 套房 | 11-1-16 |
| summer (season) | 夏天 | 夏天 | 14-2-5 |
| supermarket | 超市 | 超市 | 11-1-8 |
| to be surnamed | 姓 | 姓 | 1-1-15 |
| sweet (taste) | 甜 | 甜 | 10-1-7 |
| to swim | 游泳 | 游泳 | 3-1-9 |
| swimming pool | 游泳池 | 游泳池 | 6-2-18 |

**T**

| English definition | Traditional Characters | Simplified Characters | Lesson-Dialogue-Number |
|---|---|---|---|
| Taiwan | 臺灣 (＝台灣) | 台湾 (＝台湾) | 1-1-18 |
| Tainan, a city in southwestern Taiwan | 臺南 | 台南 | 8-1-17 |
| Taitung, name of one of the major cities on the south eastern coast of Taiwan | 臺東 | 台东 | 9-1-14 |
| to take | 帶 | 带 | 9-2-4 |
| to take (pictures) | 拍 | 拍 | 10-2-1 |

| English definition | Traditional Characters | Simplified Characters | Lesson-Dialogue-Number |
|---|---|---|---|
| to take a photo | 照相 | 照相 | 2-1-14 |
| to take a rest | 休息 | 休息 | 15-1-19 |
| to take by, to travel by | 坐 | 坐 | 8-1-1 |
| take out, to go | 外帶 | 外带 | 4-1-18 |
| to take, to require | 要 | 要 | 4-2-14 |
| tall | 高 | 高 | 10-2-10 |
| (lit. good to drink) to taste good | 好喝 | 好喝 | 1-2-5 |
| taxi | 計程車 | 出租车 | 8-2-13 |
| tea | 茶 | 茶 | 1-2-3 |
| to teach | 教 | 教 | 5-2-14 |
| teacher | 老師 | 老师 | 2-2-7 |
| teahouse | 茶館 | 茶馆 | 9-2-12 |
| telephone | 電話 | 电话 | 11-1-20 |
| ten thousand | 萬 | 万 | 4-2-15 |
| tennis | 網球 | 网球 | 3-1-6 |
| (more...) than | 比 | 比 | 8-2-8 |
| thank you | 謝謝 | 谢谢 | 1-1-22 |
| that | 那 | 那 | 4-2-10 |
| that place, there | 那裡 | 那里 | 6-1-7 |
| That's right. | 是啊 | 是啊 | 5-1-18 |
| That's very kind of you. | 太客氣 | 太客气 | 13-1-23 |
| the day after tomorrow | 後天 | 后天 | 7-1-11 |
| the same, alike | 一樣 | 一样 | 13-1-14 |
| then | 就 | 就 | 9-2-15 |
| and then | 再 | 再 | 11-1-19 |
| then | 那麼 | 那么 | 12-2-13 |
| then, in that case | 那 | 那 | 11-2-10 |
| therefore, so | 所以 | 所以 | 5-2-6 |
| these | 這些 | 这些 | 10-2-19 |
| they (used for people only) | 他們 | 他们 | 6-1-1 |
| things, stuff | 東西 | 东西 | 6-2-6 |
| to think | 想 | 想 | 11-1-18 |
| this | 這 | 这 | 1-1-12 |
| (said of self on the phone) This is s/he speaking. | 我就是 | 我就是 | 13-1-20 |
| this kind (of) | 這樣 | 这样 | 12-2-9 |

| English definition | Traditional Characters | Simplified Characters | Lesson-Dialogue-Number |
|---|---|---|---|
| this time | 這次 | 这次 | 14-2-15 |
| this year | 今年 | 今年 | 13-2-2 |
| thousand | 千 | 千 | 4-2-16 |
| throat | 喉嚨 | 喉咙 | 15-1-9 |
| to throw up, to vomit | 吐 | 吐 | 15-2-4 |
| (train, bus) ticket | 車票 | 车票 | 8-1-10 |
| time | 時間 | 时间 | 12-1-4 |
| tired | 累 | 累 | 12-1-20 |
| to | 到 | 到 | 5-2-15 |
| to | 給 | 给 | 11-1-21 |
| to | 對 | 对 | 13-2-12 |
| to | 跟 | 跟 | 15-2-11 |
| today | 今天 | 今天 | 3-2-2 |
| together | 一起 | 一起 | 3-2-13 |
| tomorrow | 明天 | 明天 | 3-1-17 |
| too | 太 | 太 | 4-2-4 |
| toward, to | 往 | 往 | 10-2-14 |
| tradition, customs | 傳統 | 传统 | 13-2-9 |
| train | 火車 | 火车 | 8-1-2 |
| to travel | 旅行 | 旅行 | 9-1-6 |
| to treat sb to sth | 請 | 请 | 10-1-14 |
| to try | 試 | 试 | 12-2-11 |
| tuition | 學費 | 学费 | 12-1-12 |
| TV | 電視 | 电视 | 9-1-4 |
| two | 兩 | 两 | 2-2-15 |
| typhoon | 颱風 | 台风 | 14-2-3 |

**U**

| | | | |
|---|---|---|---|
| umbrella | 傘 | 伞 | 14-2-2 |
| university | 大學 | 大学 | 12-1-7 |

**V**

| | | | |
|---|---|---|---|
| vacant, empty | 空 | 空 | 11-1-14 |
| verbal particle indicating a completed action | 了 | 了 | 13-2-4 |
| very | 很 | 很 | 1-2-4 |
| very | 非常 | 非常 | 8-1-11 |
| vicinity, near | 附近 | 附近 | 6-1-17 |
| Vietnam | 越南 | 越南 | 3-2-17 |
| to visit (an institution) | 參觀 | 参观 | 8-2-2 |

| English definition | Traditional Characters | Simplified Characters | Lesson-Dialogue-Number |
|---|---|---|---|
| **W** | | | |
| to wait for | 等 | 等 | 11-2-9 |
| to walk | 走路 | 走路 | 11-1-9 |
| to wander around, to look around | 逛 | 逛 | 9-2-10 |
| to want to | 要 | 要 | 1-2-13 |
| to want, to need | 要 | 要 | 4-1-9 |
| to want, to think | 想 | 想 | 3-2-7 |
| water | 水 | 水 | 15-1-18 |
| water heater | 熱水器 | 热水器 | 11-2-6 |
| watermelon | 西瓜 | 西瓜 | 10-1-9 |
| we, us | 我們 | 我们 | 1-1-10 |
| to wear, to put on | 穿 | 穿 | 10-2-4 |
| weather | 天氣 | 天气 | 14-1-1 |
| week | 星期 | 星期 | 9-1-1 |
| weekend | 週末 | 周末 | 3-1-1 |
| welcome | 歡迎 | 欢迎 | 1-1-19 |
| well known, famous | 有名 | 有名 | 5-1-7 |
| wet | 濕 | 湿 | 14-2-6 |
| what | 什麼 | 什么 | 1-2-6 |
| What's wrong? | 怎麼了 | 怎么了 | 15-2-19 |
| when | 時候 | 时候 | 7-1-10 |
| where | 哪裡 | 哪里 | 6-1-5 |
| which | 哪 | 哪 | 1-2-12 |
| Which country? | 哪國 | 哪国 | 1-2-19 |
| who | 誰 | 谁 | 2-1-17 |
| why | 為什麼 | 为什么 | 4-2-17 |
| wife | 太太 | 太太 | 10-2-7 |
| will | 會 | 会 | 11-2-8 |
| will not do | 不行 | 不行 | 8-2-12 |
| will, be going to | 要 | 要 | 14-2-4 |
| wind | 冷 | 冷 | 14-1-3 |
| window | 窗戶 | 窗户 | 10-2-13 |
| winter (season) | 冬天 | 冬天 | 14-1-10 |
| to wish (somebody happiness, good luck, etc.) | 祝 | 祝 | 13-2-13 |
| with | 跟 | 跟 | 8-1-3 |
| a woman from Taiwan | 張怡君 | 张怡君 | 2-1-1 |

| English definition | Traditional Characters | Simplified Characters | Lesson-Dialogue-Number |
|---|---|---|---|
| a woman from the US | 白如玉 | 白如玉 | 3-2-1 |
| a woman from Vietnam | 陳月美 | 陈月美 | 1-1-1 |
| to work | 工作 | 工作 | 12-2-1 |
| to write | 寫 | 写 | 7-2-17 |
| **X** | | | |
| xiaolongbao, e.g., small meat and cabbagefilled steamed buns | 小籠包 | 小笼包 | 5-1-19 |
| **Y** | | | |
| yellow | 黃色 | 黄色 | 10-1-2 |
| yes | 是的 | 是的 | 1-1-21 |
| yesterday | 昨天 | 昨天 | 5-2-1 |
| you | 你 | 你 | 1-1-4 |
| you (female) | 妳 | 妳 | 3-2-6 |
| you (honorific) | 您 | 您 | 2-2-3 |
| you (plural) | 你們 | 你们 | 1-1-17 |
| You're welcome. | 不客氣 | 不客气 | 1-1-22 |
| young | 年輕 | 年轻 | 13-2-10 |
| younger brother | 弟弟 | 弟弟 | 10-2-11 |
| younger sister | 妹妹 | 妹妹 | 2-1-19 |
| Yu Shan (Mount Jade), tallest mountain in central Taiwan | 玉山 | 玉山 | 14-1-15 |

### 第六课　他们学校在山上

**对话一**

安　同：听说怡君的学校很漂亮。
如　玉：他们学校在哪里？远不远？
安　同：有一点远。他们学校在花莲的山上。
如　玉：山上？那里的风景一定很美。
安　同：是的，他们学校前面有海，后面有山，那里真的是一个很漂亮的地方。
如　玉：我想去看看。我们这个周末一起去吧！
安　同：好啊！我现在要去学校附近的咖啡店买咖啡。妳呢？
如　玉：我去楼下找朋友，我们要一起去上课。

**对话二**

怡　君：欢迎你们来。
安　同：你们学校真远！
怡　君：是啊，不是很近，有一点不方便。
如　玉：这里的学生在哪里买东西？
怡　君：在学校外面。学校里面没有商店。
安　同：吃饭呢？学校里面有没有餐厅？
怡　君：有，餐厅在学生宿舍的一楼。
安　同：前面这栋大楼很漂亮。
怡　君：这是图书馆，旁边的那栋大楼是教室，图书馆后面有游泳池。

### 第七课　早上九点去KTV

**对话一**

安　同：月美，妳要去哪里？
月　美：去KTV唱歌。我和朋友九点二十分在大安KTV见面。
安　同：早上九点去KTV？为什么？
月　美：从早上七点到中午十二点，最便宜。要不要一起去？
安　同：我想去，可是我得去银行。下次吧！
月　美：好啊，下次你一定要来，我想听你唱歌。
安　同：没问题。对了，什么时候有空一起吃饭？
月　美：后天我有空，你呢？
安　同：我也有空，后天晚上七点怎么样？
月　美：好啊！再见。

**对话二**

安　同：如玉，妳在吃饭啊？
如　玉：是，吃午餐，等一下要上课。你呢？
安　同：我刚下课。对了，下午四点半学校有篮球比赛。妳想去看吗？
如　玉：想啊。比赛几点结束？
安　同：六点半。妳晚上有事吗？
如　玉：我最近很忙，每天晚上都上书法课。

安　同：学得怎么样？
如　玉：刚开始学，字写得不好，可是我觉得很有意思。
安　同：我有空可以去看看吗？
如　玉：我得问问老师。

### 第八课　坐火车去台南

**对话一**

如　玉：这个周末，我想跟朋友去台南玩。
明　华：怎么去？
如　玉：我想坐火车去。
明　华：火车太慢了，要四个多钟头，坐高铁比较快。
如　玉：可是听说高铁车票非常贵。
明　华：高铁车票有一点贵，但是坐高铁又快又舒服。
如　玉：我不知道在哪里买票。
明　华：在高铁站、网路上或是便利商店都可以。
如　玉：这么方便！那我坐高铁去，谢谢你。

**对话二**

如　玉：安同，明天我们没课，你想去哪里？
安　同：我要跟同学去参观故宫博物院。
如　玉：听说那里有很多中国古代的东西。
安　同：是啊。妳要跟我们去看看吗？
如　玉：好。怎么去？
安　同：我同学骑机车载我。妳可以坐公共汽车去。
如　玉：我想坐捷运去。比较快。
安　同：不行，到故宫没有捷运。妳要不要坐计程车去？
如　玉：太贵了！我坐公车。骑机车比坐公车快吗？
安　同：差不多。

### 第九课　放假去哪里玩？

**对话一**

安　同：田中，下个星期我们放五天的假，你要回国吗？
田　中：不，我打算在家看电视、影片学中文，你呢？
安　同：我想跟朋友去玩。
田　中：不错啊。去什么地方？
安　同：台东。听说那里的风景非常漂亮。
田　中：我也听说。放假的时候，你常去旅行吗？
安　同：不一定。有时候在家写功课，有时候出去玩。

田　　中：你们什么时候去台东？
安　　同：这个星期六下午去。
田　　中：去玩多久？
安　　同：大概玩四、五天。

**对话二**

田　　中：我女朋友九月三十号要来台湾看我。
明　　华：你想带她去哪里玩？
田　　中：还不知道。你有什么建议？
明　　华：台湾的夜市很有名。你们应该去逛逛。
田　　中：谢谢，还有什么好玩的地方？
明　　华：台湾的茶也很特别。台北有很多茶馆。
田　　中：到哪里喝茶比较好？
明　　华：你们可以去猫空。那里的风景很美。
田　　中：谢谢你。我决定带她去猫空。你也一起去，好不好？
明　　华：要是那时候我有空，就跟你们一起去。
田　　中：太好了！谢谢！

## 第十课　台湾的水果很好吃

**对话一**

如　　玉：这个黄色的水果叫什么？
月　　美：芒果。给你一块，吃吃看。
如　　玉：好，谢谢。**[taking a bite]** 香香的、甜甜的，很好吃。
月　　美：昨天明华给我们的那种水果，红色的，叫什么？
如　　玉：你說的是西瓜吧？
月　　美：对！对！对！台湾有很多好吃的水果。
如　　玉：我以前不喜欢吃水果，现在很喜欢了。
月　　美：越南的水果也很好吃。
如　　玉：要是有机会，我想吃吃看。
月　　美：你来越南，我一定请你吃。

**对话二**

明　　华：你跟你女朋友上个月去花莲玩，好玩吗？
田　　中：很好玩。你看，这些是我拍的照片。
明　　华：你们笑得很开心！哪一个是你女朋友？
田　　中：穿红衣服的这个。穿黄衣服的是旅馆老板的太太。
明　　华：她们两个都很漂亮。这两个男的是谁？
田　　中：矮的是旅馆老板，高的是他弟弟。
明　　华：那家旅馆怎么样？
田　　中：很干净。从窗户往外看，是蓝色的大海。
明　　华：真不错！那家旅馆贵吗？
田　　中：因为现在去玩的人比较少，所以旅馆不太贵。
明　　华：下次我也想去住。

Linking Chinese

# 當代中文課程　課本 1-2（二版）

| | | | | |
|---|---|---|---|---|
| 策　　劃 | 國立臺灣師範大學國語教學中心 | 發 行 人 | 林載爵 |
| 主　　編 | 鄧守信 | 社　　長 | 羅國俊 |
| 顧　　問 | Claudia Ross、白建華、陳雅芬 | 總 經 理 | 陳芝宇 |
| 審　　查 | 姚道中、葉德明、劉珣 | 總 編 輯 | 涂豐恩 |
| 編寫教師 | 王佩卿、陳慶華、黃桂英 | 副總編輯 | 陳逸華 |
| 英文審查 | 李櫻、畢永峨 | | |

| | | | |
|---|---|---|---|
| 執行編輯 | 張莉萍、張雯雯、張黛琪、蔡如珮 | 叢書編輯 | 賴祖兒 |
| 英文翻譯 | 范大龍、張克微、蔣宜臻、龍潔玉 | 地　　址 | 新北市汐止區大同路一段 369 號 1 樓 |
| 校　　對 | 張莉萍、張雯雯、張黛琪、蔡如珮、 | 聯絡電話 | (02)8692-5588 轉 5305 |
| | 李芃、鄭秀娟 | 郵政劃撥 | 帳戶第 0100559-3 號 |
| 編輯助理 | 許雅晴、喬愛淳 | 郵撥電話 | (02)23620308 |
| 技術支援 | 李昆璟 | 印 刷 者 | 文聯彩色製版印刷有限公司 |
| 插　　畫 | 何慎修、張榮傑、黃奕穎 | | 2021 年 10 月初版・2024 年 9 月初版第十刷 |
| 封面設計 | Lady Gugu | | 版權所有・翻印必究 |
| 內文排版 | 洪伊珊 | | Printed in Taiwan. |
| 錄　　音 | 王育偉、王品超、李世揚、吳霈蓁、 | ISBN | 978-957-08-5970-6 (平裝) |
| | 馬君珮、許伯琴、Michael Tennant | GPN | 1011001470 |
| 錄音後製 | 純粹錄音後製公司 | 定　　價 | 400 元 |

著作財產權人　國立臺灣師範大學
地址：臺北市和平東路一段 162 號
電話：886-2-7749-5130
網址：http://mtc.ntnu.edu.tw/
E-mail：mtcbook613@gmail.com

感謝

王佩卿、王盈婷、王盈雯、何瑞章、李尚遠、林欣穎、林聖雄、林媽芳、林蔚儒、徐國欽、張素華、
張瑜庭、莊淑帆、陳宇婕、陳冠引、陳建宏、陳昱蓉、陳韋誠、陳書韋、陳淑美、陳逸達、陳嘉禧、
陳鳳儀、傅聖芳、黃奕穎、楊凌雁、虞永欣、蔡宛蓉、賴瑩玲
協助拍攝本教材及試用教材期間使用之相關照片

udn TV、中央氣象局、《中國顏色》（黃仁達／著、攝）、台北 101、台灣大車隊、
《台灣喫茶》（吳德亮／著、攝）、統一超商、蕙風堂、聯合報
授權提供本教材之相關照片

（以上依姓氏或單位名稱筆畫順序排列）

國家圖書館出版品預行編目資料

當代中文課程 課本 1-2（二版）/國立臺灣師範大學國語
教學中心策劃．鄧守信主編．初版．新北市．聯經．
2021 年 10 月．164 面．21×28 公分（Linking Chiese）
ISBN　978-957-08-5970-6（平裝）
[2024 年 9 月初版第十刷]

1.漢語　2.讀本

802.86　　　　　　　　　　　　　　　　　110012624